Mill

Best Seller Romance

A chance to read and collect some of the best-loved novels from Mills & Boon—the world's largest publisher of romantic fiction.

Every month, six titles by favourite Mills & Boon authors will be re-published in the *Best Seller Romance* series.

A list of other titles in the *Best Seller Romance* series can be found at the end of this book.

Margaret Pargeter

RIDE A
BLACK HORSE

MILLS & BOON LIMITED
LONDON · TORONTO

First published 1975
Australian copyright 1982
Philippine copyright 1982
This edition 1982

© Margaret Pargeter 1975

ISBN 0 263 74137 0

Set in 10 on 11pt Times

02-1282

*Made and printed in Great Britain by
Richard Clay (The Chaucer Press) Ltd,
Bungay, Suffolk*

CHAPTER I

The advertisement read: Girl Friday required for general duties on large estate. Able to ride and drive. Only those really in need of a job and interested in hard work need apply.

Jane stared at it again as she propped the newspaper in front of her on the ledge of the hotel telephone booth. The advertisement, economical in structure, bluntly frank in context, seemed to hold her gaze magnetically. It constituted a challenge, along with other things. Carefully she marked the place with a pencil, then picking up the telephone slowly dialled the number which was given at the end. The code for the address was pinned up on the wall beside the directory. She had no difficulty at all getting through.

The line buzzed for a few seconds before anyone answered her call. 'This is High Linton, 315,' a deeply toned feminine voice announced ponderously. 'Manager's House.'

'Oh. Good morning . . .' Jane stumbled, suddenly confused, as her mind went curiously blank. Her preconceived little speech seemed to have flown from her head. She couldn't think of anything to say. 'Perhaps I'd better speak to the manager, if he's in?' she managed at last. 'It's about the vacancy in this morning's *Journal*. My name is Jane Browne, and I would like to apply.'

There came a long pause while the woman at the other end of the line obviously considered this bit of information. Then she said slowly, 'I haven't seen the paper yet, but I expect Mr Grierson is advertising again. He's the boss, and I know he wants somebody. The manager is away today, and Mrs Tate, the housekeeper, is out too. However, I suppose it will be all right if you

7

care to come along. Mr Grierson might see you himself if you come straight away.'

The woman didn't give her name, and Jane had a frightening premonition that the receiver at High Linton was about to be dropped immediately. 'Please,' she spoke swiftly, 'where do I find you?'

'Find me . . .? the woman repeated anxiously. 'Oh, you mean where do you come to? Yes, I suppose you'll need to know that. Well, I can tell you how to get here if you have a pencil handy, but mind you, it's not an easy place to find!'

'And you can say that again,' Jane muttered darkly to herself, as some time later she watched the bus on which she had travelled disappearing from sight along the deserted country road. She had taken the train as instructed, from Newcastle to Haydon Bridge, then, after a long wait, had caught a local bus to this road-end. Altogether the whole operation seemed to have taken much longer than it should have done. The countryside looked wild and bleak, and where High Linton could be she couldn't imagine. From where she stood there was no sign of a dwelling of any kind!

To add to her depression, the idea of being interviewed by the owner of the estate was rather frightening. She might, she thought, have stood a much better chance of impressing a modern young manager. This Mr Grierson was probably a fussy, elderly man who might consider anyone under forty unsuitable.

Rather reluctantly she was beginning to wonder if she had been too impulsive. It was, she knew, one of her worst faults, although she would rather die than admit it. It was enough that her father was always lecturing her about it. Not that he was adverse to taking risks himself. He wouldn't have been so wealthy today if he had not. But this wasn't the same as being impulsive, or so he said.

Jane sighed as she slung her leather handbag casually

over her shoulder and started off down the narrow road, following the brief directions of the kindly bus driver. Once started on anything she always felt honour bound, if only to her own principles, to see it through. She was definitely taking a risk this afternoon, but a risk which she was convinced must in some way be related to fate. The same fate which had been responsible for the break-down of her car yesterday as she was leaving Newcastle on her way to Edinburgh. It had happened near the large hotel where she'd been forced to spend the night, and where she had arranged to stay until a nearby garage could get the necessary spare parts to fix her sports model for her.

Otherwise she would never have seen a local news-paper. Actually she hadn't purchased the one she had looked at herself. It had been lying in one of the hotel lounges, and she had picked it up and carried it to her breakfast table. Someone had left it already folded on the back page with its columns of vacancies. She had merely glanced at it idly as she'd drunk her orange juice.

The boxed advertisement had caught her attention straight away. A job in the country! It was something she had always wanted, ever since she had left board-ing school. There she had dreamt of having a riding school of her own, with a small acreage of land for her horses. It hadn't seemed too much to hope for, but such ambitions were doomed to a quick death. Eustace Browne, her father, might own factories and have money to spare, but he refused to have anything to do with such a scheme.

'I'm not throwing good money away, Jane,' he had said, the inherent thrift passed down through genera-tions of Yorkshire business men still firmly entrenched in his blood. Look after the pennies, was his favourite quotation, and the pounds will look after themselves.

Which hadn't helped her much, Jane thought grimly, as she remembered how all her pleading had failed to move him. Now, three years later, she could also remember her own bitterness. How, although almost eighteen, she had found it quite beyond her to retaliate effectively. Possibly owing to her rather sheltered existence she had no idea how to cope with a man of her father's calibre.

And neither had his attitude changed over the years. Jane's expensive education, with its bonus of wealthy contacts, he had considered an investment, but a riding school, even a small one, could cost a fortune and, in the hands of an inexperienced girl, could be a disaster. If she wanted to do something she could come into the factory.

Jane had known all along that he had wanted her in the factory. Often she felt that he had never really forgiven her for not being a boy. With his large business empire Eustace could have done with half a dozen sons. Instead, he had only one.

Jane's brother George was ten years older than herself and had been pulling his weight for years. Eustace could see no reason why Jane shouldn't do the same. In a different capacity, of course. Rebelliously, without stopping to really consider, Jane had thrust her ambitions into cold storage, determined to show him that she wasn't just a scatterbrained young dreamer. After completing a secretarial course she had worked hard, and was now assistant personal secretary to one of the directors. She possessed a quick brain and an aptitude for figures which delighted her father, but secretly depressed his daughter who could find little enthusiasm within herself for the work.

It might have helped, she had often said, if they had lived in the country, but both her parents were so content in their luxurious town house that it would have taken an earthquake to move them.

It wasn't as if her father had actively stopped her from finding other work, but previously his subtle and strong personality had proved an active if invisible deterrent. But lately Jane's own personality had been developing and sparks had started to fly. She disturbed an otherwise serene domestic atmosphere. Her mother conformed, George conformed, but Jane found she could not. She was discovering a certain wilfulness. A strong desire to escape the conventional routine warred with her former strivings to remain on good terms with her family. A growing rebelliousness invaded Jane's restless spirit to the extent that she changed her mind about taking her annual holiday with her parents in Canada as arranged.

With a rueful shrug she trudged on down the apparently endless road. There had been a fearful row when she had told them. Eustace had completely lost his temper, and told her in no uncertain terms that she was thoroughly spoilt. That she was too used to having her own way and if she ever married he hoped it would be to a man who could give her a proper good hiding when she needed it. His blunt, north country temper was never suppressed when he had something to say!

Jane sniffed wryly, as she tossed back her hair. She couldn't help feeling that on this occasion he had been rather unfair. Hadn't she just helped her mother through a long tedious illness, relieving and assisting her nurse, and doing all sorts of tiresome chores about the house without grumbling? As for a future husband—Pops had a nerve! Wasn't he doing everything possible to marry her off to a man who, in her opinion, wasn't capable of anything very much?

Felix Browne was a distant cousin whom Eustace had incorporated into the firm, and Jane could quite see, or thought she did, that by marrying Felix she could help spread the Brownes out a bit, especially as George and his wife had no family, as yet. But, in spite of her resistance, she couldn't rid herself of the notion that if she didn't escape soon she might find herself coerced into an engagement whether she wanted it or not.

Surrounded by clouds of disapproval Jane had seen her parents off at Heathrow. They would be away almost two months while Eustace toured business interests in Canada and visited relations whom he hadn't seen for years. Her mother seemed as excited as a schoolgirl about it all and not unduly put out that Jane wasn't going with them. She was probably delighted to have her husband to herself for a time, Jane had decided, feeling slightly happier as she had watched the huge Trident jet disappear against the horizon.

On her way home she had decided suddenly to spend her own holiday in Scotland. A school friend, whose parents had a villa in St Tropez, had been in touch, inviting her to join the family out there. And yet another, whose brother was going to be short-handed on his yacht, begged her to come and help out, but she had refused both these invitations, though quite unable to say why as she liked France and sailing very much. She had never been to Scotland before, or even as far north as she was now. This was why she felt, perhaps irrationally, that there had been a touch of destiny about these last few days. A peculiar weaving of circumstances which had led her inevitably to this lonely country road in the wild border country of Northumberland.

'I think I'm lost!' She spoke aloud again, as there was no one to hear her and the sound of a voice, even her own brought comfort. She wasn't used to such bare open spaces. Just as she was beginning to think that she had been wrongly directed, she saw a house. A house and some other buildings, half hidden behind a group of tall trees. As she walked past the trees she saw that the house was large and squarely built of grey stone, obviously the farmhouse, it stood well back from the road, slightly apart from the other buildings and steading, and a board with the farm's name printed across it swung from a high pillar at the end of the drive.

So this was High Linton. The gravel drive, judging from its length, apparently led to another residence of some size. Ignoring this, Jane turned off along a stone-flagged path which she followed around to the back of the farmhouse and knocked tentatively on the weather-beaten door.

After several minutes, just as she was about to turn away, she heard heavy footsteps, and the door was opened carefully by a large, over-made woman. Jane was immediately certain that this was the person she had spoken to earlier on the telephone.

'I'm sorry to have kept you waiting,' the woman panted breathlessly. 'I heard you knocking, but I was upstairs making the beds. We're all behind today, you see, as the housekeeper is away. Did you want to see Mrs Tate?' Her small, bright eyes stared Jane curiously up and down.

Sensing that the woman felt flustered, Jane smiled and hastened to reassure her. 'I think I spoke to you this morning? I rang about a job. You advised me to come right away, so I caught the next train. I'm Jane Browne.'

'Oh, yes.' Far from her being reassured the woman's frown deepened as she added cautiously, 'It was me who answered. I'm Mrs Dick, the stockman's wife. But I only work here part-time and couldn't really advise you much about the job you're after. And, as I've just said, Mrs Tate is out.'

Jane glanced at her, bewildered, and although she kept smiling she had a feeling that the smile was fixed to her face. She tried again. 'If I remember, you did say that a Mr Grierson might see me? Or if this is impossible I can always wait and see the manager, or Mrs Tate when she returns.'

Mrs Dick continued to look apprehensive. 'I only hope I did right,' she exclaimed, her brown eyes staring uncertainly at Jane's smooth face. 'I hope you aren't one of these society girls come to waste Mr Grierson's

13

time!'

Jane felt a quick stab of dismay tinged with indignation which she tried hard to suppress. What was Mrs Dick talking about? How had she got the impression that she was anything but a working girl? Besides, all girls worked these days, regardless of class. She wasn't aware that in her blue denim trews and jacket she was as slim and as straight as a boy, but with an indefinable air of breeding about her which was partly responsible for Mrs Dick's uneasiness.

' I'm sorry,' she said at last, with just a trace of impatience. ' I wouldn't be here if I intended wasting Mr Grierson's time!'

Fortunately Mrs Dick didn't appear to notice Jane's slight irritation, or that she had only half answered her question. Her frown smoothed out and she relaxed, even to the extent of permitting herself a small smile. ' Well,' she said grudgingly, ' you don't seem to be such an uppish young lady as the last one we had. Only I feel sort of responsible, you see, and I don't want to get into Mr Grierson's black books! If you would care to step inside I'll go and see if I can find him about the stables. If not then you'll just have to go up to the big house yourself and see if he's there.'

This Mr Grierson must be quite a tyrant, Jane decidedly nervously, as she followed Mrs Dick into the house. Mrs Dick seemed rather scared of him. A sharp prickle of foreboding ran down Jane's spine. ' It's very good of you to bother,' she murmured conventionally, as Mrs Dick showed her into a small study and closed the door.

Although the outside of the house seemed stark and uncompromising, inside it was completely different. In the study a log fire burnt cheerfully in spite of the warmth of the early September day, and deep, brown leather armchairs stood invitingly at either side of the wide hearth. A desk stood against the wall at the other end of the room with papers and account books piled neatly on top of it. Jane glanced appreciatively around as she sat down with rather a weary sigh in one of the chairs. If this was the manager's house he probably used this room as his office, and very cosy he must be, too.

Her eyes went slowly around to the window. Outside the fields lay serene in the late summer sunshine. Trees massed in the hedgerows, taking the bareness from land ringed by wire fences and stone walls, and cattle stood beneath them, swishing their tails at the occasional fly. Tynedale, she had noticed, was wooded, with gentle green stretches, yet, on the way here, Jane had caught glimpses of a wilder landscape and hills rising stark and bleak against the sky-line. She had a sudden, uneasy feeling that this latter impression was more truly characteristic of the county she hoped to work in. Not the gently undulating scene she was looking out on now.

Considering everything, it seemed a good place to hide from the increasing pressure of her father's scheming, And if she did get this job it might prove, once and for all, where her true vocation lay.

The warm glow from the fire was soothing. Jane, tired from her busy morning, lay back in her chair, willing herself to relax before someone came in, not able to account for a definite twinge of nervousness. After a few minutes, the silence and the heat from the fire had the desired effect and she almost fell asleep.

'Good afternoon.'

The single word of greeting was flung sharply. Startled, Jane opened her eyes and sat up with a jerk. She hadn't heard anyone come in! Now she found herself regarded narrowly by a pair of piercing dark eyes. Dark grey eyes. Unable to look away, she stared into them hypnotically. They were set in a hard brown face beneath heavy brows. A tall man, lean but powerfully built, with dark, very definite features. Not exactly

15

young any more. Somewhere, she assessed, between thirty and forty, it would be difficult to tell exactly, but he definitely wasn't the elderly employer she had envisaged.

Shock, which afterwards she couldn't account for, held her immobile. She sat quite still in her chair, locked by a curious tension, conscious that her pulse was jerking in a totally unpredictable manner. Bewildered, she flickered her thick lashes nervously as she tried to pull herself together. Didn't she meet all kinds of men at the factory—every day? One man, vital and forceful he might seem, was surely not enough to throw a girl off balance?

His eyes seemed to leap over her as he said sardonically, ' When you've quite woken up perhaps you could take off that ridiculous hat, then we might get down to business. My name is Grierson, Karl Grierson, and I own this place. Hilda tells me that you're here about a job?'

Jane choked as his words jerked her upright. She couldn't remember anyone, except perhaps her father, speaking to her exactly like that before! Warm colour tinted her face as her hand went defensively to her head. It was her favourite khaki-coloured hat, and its wide brim hid her tightly braided, copper-dark hair. She had fixed it firmly, pinning it down before she left town, feeling instinctively that the plainer her appearance the better her chances of success. She wasn't aware of the piquant appeal of the part of her face visible beneath the shadowed brim. The warmth of her colouring, the curve of her mouth, the unconscious promise of beauty held rigidly in check.

Her wide almond green eyes sparkled indignantly, registering her dismay as she retorted faintly, still clutching her hat, ' If you don't mind I'd rather keep it on.'

' As you like.' He didn't argue, just shrugged his

16

wide shoulders indifferently, his dark brows lifting fractionally as his grey eyes probed her green ones. 'I might even find it a novelty to interview a nose and a mouth.'

His own rather sensuous mouth quirked as he turned to remove his light tweed jacket, throwing it with expert aim to a peg on the wall, before walking across and seating himself casually behind the manager's desk. When he moved the well cut shirt he wore stretched across the hard muscles of his chest.

Jane stayed silent, crouched in her chair, watching him compulsively as he studied some notes on a pad in front of him. The light from the window glanced off his face, revealing a certain pride and ruthlessness. The face of a tycoon! A man used to giving orders and being obeyed. Lord of all before him! The comparison leapt to Jane's mind, bringing a smouldering resentment. Her slender boneless body went taut. Was there really such a thing as jumping from the frying pan into the fire? She was struck by an uneasy suspicion that in this man ran some of the same qualities which motivated her father! Surely, in spite of all her endeavour, she hadn't come full circle, to meet the very thing she was running away from!

She wondered that he had bothered to see her at all, even though Mrs Dick had sought him out. If his manager had been around he probably wouldn't have given her a second thought. In a way it was rather like her father having to interview a tea-boy. While such condescension didn't please Jane one bit, the thought caused her temporary amusement.

The scrape of Karl Grierson's chair banished all such frivolities from her mind as he turned to survey her again. With a speculative gleam in his eyes he tapped the pad he was holding with one decisive finger. 'I believe,' he said drily, 'you saw my advertisement in this morning's paper, and that you would like to work here?'

The directness of his opening gambit caught her unawares. Confusion swept through her as she heard herself reply in a completely muddled fashion. 'Yes, I rang, and Mrs Dick said to come along. So I came . . .' She didn't need to look at his sardonic face to realize that he was completely unimpressed by the pointlessness of her naïve remarks.

'Just like that.' His voice changed slightly on a note of dry irony. 'Usually I don't appreciate people who waste my time.'

'You don't have to make an exception of me.' Because she was annoyed with herself for being so inane, the sharply defensive retort was out before she could stop it.

His cool, level gaze was devastating. 'Nothing,' he said suavely, 'could be further from my mind.'

The air seemed suddenly static. Jane flushed, twisting her head away, feeling helplessly that she was rapidly reducing any chance of getting the job she was after.

'I'm sorry.' Her flush deepened, annoyed as much by her own stupidity as his ability to make her feel gauche. She sat very still, scarcely breathing. He was too darkly, vividly masculine! The thought depressed and excited her at once, two conflicting emotions, and the shock to her heart was sudden, constricting. She said, too quickly, 'If you're busy I can wait and see your manager when he returns. I don't suppose you usually bother about the domestic staff.'

Inexplicably his voice rang, bringing her eyes sharply back to his face. 'The whole of my domestic staff concerns me, Miss—er—Jane Browne, I think Hilda said?'

As Jane nodded, confused, he went on with emphasis, 'I work in conjunction with my manager, Miss Browne, and I like to know whom we're employing. I farm almost two thousand acres, so you can understand how important it is that I can rely on each member of my

18

staff.'

His voice had a ring of sincerity and, against her will, she responded, although an appropriately bright comment eluded her. She tried desperately to emulate his ease and sophistication. 'I take it that you don't think I would be suitable?'

He shot her a look very difficult to define. 'I haven't said that—not yet!'

She looked away from that dark, sardonic face. 'But you aren't impressed . . . '

'You jump too quickly to conclusions.' He flickered an impatient glance over her averted profile. Something in his expression as she glanced back a him made her feel utterly ridiculous. 'Suppose,' he suggested smoothly, 'that you stop being so vulnerable, and we start again?'

Squashing a rising sense of mutiny, she waited in silent, if not very willing agreement. A new impulse, which boosted her sense of the ridiculous, urged her to jump up and walk out. It took a great deal of resolution to remain seated in her chair.

He flicked her a rather crooked smile, satirical, a shade curt, as if he guessed her reactions and almost matched them with his own. 'I'm presuming that you don't live in these parts? I certainly can't remember seeing you before.'

'No,' Jane's heavy lashes flickered uncertainly on her pale cheeks. How could she possibly hope to avoid the issue? She had been foolish to imagine that such a contingency wouldn't arise. She said slowly, concentrating on the softly patterned carpet, 'I live near Bradford. I just happened to be up north on holiday.' With returning confidence her delicately rounded chin came up. No need to elaborate at this stage, she decided, meeting his sharp glance squarely.

'And you suddenly decide that you'll work here?' He was regarding her steadily. 'Yet you know nothing of the locality. Have you ever even been on a farm, I wonder?'

Her newly found assurance was transitory. Again her lashes flickered over guarded green eyes, while a sense of inescapable disaster settled in her mind. She replied evasively, ' I like horses, and the country. I'm sure I should suit you very well.'

' Indeed!' His dark eyebrows rose as he surveyed her sceptically. ' Over the past months we've had several young ladies of the same opinion, and unfortunately they have all been wrong.'

' Surely . . .'

He cut off her half-formed protest abruptly. ' Some of them probably had more money than sense. After the last one I resolved to inquire a little closer into their background. Might I ask what your father does?'

Jane froze, her lips suddenly dry, and she moistened them cautiously with the tip of her tongue. She wanted to pretend she hadn't heard, but it was too late. A dangerous light seemed to flicker in his eyes as he waited for her reply, a light which proclaimed quite clearly that evasion was impossible. But which also convinced her that her reply would directly influence her chance of getting this job. Obviously, and, she thought, unfairly, he had made up his mind that his next employee should have no pretensions to wealth of any kind, and she would certainly be spelling out her own finale if she admitted to such.

Inwardly fuming, she brushed the back of her hand across her hot brow, unaware that the man sitting opposite her put an entirely different construction on the slight tremor in her voice as she murmured starkly, ' My father is a working man.' Fundamentally it was quite true.

His frown was swift, and impatient. ' There's nothing wrong with that. Don't look so guilty. We are all in that category today. It's your ability to work that chiefly concerns me. What have you been doing re-

20

cently?'

Jane had the breathless feeling that she was jumping hurdles. The last she had scraped over with luck, but could she hope to be so lucky next time? He had concluded that her father did some menial task, and wouldn't embarrass her by probing for details. Trying to think straight, she stared at his dark face. 'I've been working in an office,' she confessed briefly. Then, with a rush, 'I didn't like it. It's not quite my thing, but I can ride quite well and look after a house. My mother was ill recently and I looked after her . . .'

'And now that she has recovered you are looking for a different sort of job?' His cool, level gaze, though slightly more tolerant, was still wary as she nodded her head. 'Where did you learn to ride?' he asked, leaning towards her fractionally across the table, and she sensed he attached some importance to her answer.

Jane gulped. It might not be wise to mention Linda, her best friend at school, and with whom she had regularly spent some of the long school holidays. Her father, John Grant, the famous racehorse owner, had taught her all she knew. He'd used to tell her that she was a 'natural.' At one time she had thought of asking for a job in his stable, but had been chary of approaching family friends.

Now she replied rather vaguely, 'I did have proper tuition. Perhaps you would like to see me ride?'

'In a few minutes,' his dark eyes glinted thoughtfully. 'At least on that point you seem fairly confident, but I presume that your actual experience on farms is nil?'

'I suppose so.' Her head dropped a little, but she added defiantly, 'I do have my share of common sense.'

His eyes slipped over her downbent head. 'Some experience does help.' His voice stung with extreme dryness.

Jane shivered, feeling the onslaught of his derisive

21

eyes before looking up to meet his narrowed glance. Curiously shaken by her own inadequacy, swiftly she lowered her heavy lashes again, afraid that he should catch a glimpse of her sudden despair. She sensed his extraordinary perception and was aware that at that moment she had few weapons with which to fight him. Perhaps her only hope lay in the picture she had inadvertently painted of a poor girl desperately in need of employment. If she had managed to arouse his sympathy, he might decide to give her a chance?

Abruptly the uneven swivel of his chair broke the taut silence. She stared at him with trancelike concentration as he said cynically, 'You might be a brilliant rider, but I must convince myself that you do know one end of the horse from the other before I employ you. While we're away Hilda will make you a pot of tea. You could probably do with it.' His eyes on her pale, tense face were half amused, half irritated.

Her breath caught as she scrambled quickly to her feet, following him blindly as he rose and leading the way from the house. 'Thank you, Mr Grierson,' she said to the back of his dark head, surprised to find she was trembling a little. 'I'm sure I won't disappoint you.'

'We'll see,' he retorted crisply, slowing a little, waiting for her to catch up, and when she did, watching with interest her futile attempts to match his long strides.

Almost hating him, Jane ran after him on numbed feet. It was better to keep moving. Away from those eyes! Overhead clouds gathered, heralding night. She hadn't realized it was so late! Looking hastily at her watch, she saw that it was after seven o'clock and, as yet, she had made no arrangements for getting back to town. The last bus had probably long since gone. However, what did a small thing like that matter if her plans were going to succeed? With returning optimism she almost smiled at Karl Grierson's broad back.

She saw how he glanced around him as he walked, keenly observant. They walked silently, weaving their way through a comprehensive assortment of farm buildings and woodland, which must have covered several acres, until they came to a long line of looseboxes and whitewashed stables. Everything, Jane noticed, was clinically clean.

His eyes were on her, suavely considering, as he opened the door of one of the stables, taking a rope from a peg. Jane waited, warm colour tinting her cheekbones, as he disappeared into the harness room and returned with a light saddle under his arm. 'You can close the door behind me,' he said.

Jane did as she was told, her fingers fortunately nimble beneath his analytical eyes. His rapier glance missed nothing, vividly weighing and assessing her every move. There was nothing that he would overlook, and the knowledge brought a faint, if reprehensible, hostility.

In a field behind the stables two hunters grazed with a young mare. The mare, almost as if aware of an audience, was racing against the wind, all flowing mane and flying tail, and flickering sensitive ears. The other two horses, seeing her go, gave chase. Over the dry grass Jane could hear the heavy thud of their hooves and see their shining muscles rippling in the evening sun.

As they drew nearer, Karl Grierson called twice, and the mare obediently trotted towards him tossing her head, blowing delicately through her nostrils. All gleaming gold, her wide eyes watchful yet curious, she edged closer, thrusting forward her damp muzzle for a sugar lump which he produced from his pocket. 'She's very biddable, you'll find,' he commented, gently patting the slender arched neck, glancing enigmatically at Jane's eager face. 'We'll just have the saddle on and see what you can do.'

The mare obviously knew men and trusted them, and

23

it was clear that she adored him. Jane smiled for the first time as she felt a familiar growing elation inside her. She spoke to the mare quietly, giving her time to become a little more familiar. John Grant used to say that one shouldn't hurry a horse at this stage.

'Her name is Guinevere.' Karl Grierson supplied the information just as she was about to ask.

'Queen Guinevere, wife of King Arthur,' Jane mused softly, unaware that the man glanced at her sharply. 'Why, she's more like a princess!'

'I'm afraid I didn't have much say in the matter,' he smiled coolly. 'She was a year old when she came here and already had a name.'

'It seems rather ponderous, too matronly.'

'I can assure you that there's nothing ponderous about her ride,' he replied drily.

He edged the mare around, passing Jane the reins, his manner clearly indicating that he considered the conversation tedious. Within seconds she found herself up in the saddle and away, galloping over the springing turf, the reins held lightly, the wind cool on her flushed face.

'Take it easy!' he called after her, but she scarcely heard.

Exhilaration surged. Because of her mother's illness it was a long time since Jane had been on a horse. Too long, she acknowledged, feeling the expertise in her slim nervous fingers. Nervous because Karl Grierson watched her! Then she forgot about him, lost in her own intense pleasure as the sound of Guinevere's hooves rose like music to her ears. They skimmed over the ground, barely seeming to touch the grass as they galloped to the other side of the field.

'You're beautiful!' Jane breathed aloud, leaning over the satiny neck. And the mare pricked up her ears, pleased with the compliment, receiving it royally as her due. Jane laughed happily, pulling Guinevere to a canter as returning they approached a long line of hurdles. With incredible smoothness they sailed over each one of them, landing neatly on the other side. The girl's lips moved slightly, emitting a blissful sigh. Then, all her senses alive, the horse responding to the slightest movement of hands and heel, she rode swiftly back to where Karl Grierson stood waiting beside the gate.

CHAPTER II

Jane approached Karl Grierson cautiously, aware of a certain apprehension. So far she seemed to have made little impression and she found it increasingly difficult to retain even a modicum of self-assurance. Even if she had managed a fairly competent performance, he might not be altogether satisfied?

She sensed rather than saw his surprise, but she was instantly aware of her own when he said curtly as she slipped down beside him, 'I guess you'll do. If you can manage your other chores half as well, I won't complain.'

His voice was ironical, tinged with satire, and Jane blinked up at him uncertainly as she passed him the reins. Guinevere edged in between them, bumping her away. Desperately she strove for composure as she followed him from the field. 'Does that mean that I'm hired?' she asked, as his gaze slewed over her drily.

'You could say that,' he affirmed smoothly, a depth of mockery in his dark, slanting eyes.

She murmured her thanks rather breathlessly, clutching her hat which was still miraculously glued to her head. But from beneath the floppy brim tendrils of hair had escaped, caressing her cheeks like strands of burnished fire, contrasting vividly with the clear green of her eyes. 'I . . . Thank you very much,' she repeated awkwardly.

'Forget it.' His well cut mouth quirked at the corners, as if he derived some sort of amusement from her few stilted words, as if her attempted humility had not escaped him. 'You might even live to regret it.'

Did his voice hold some hint of a threat? Jane told herself firmly not to be so ridiculous, but her feet stumbled as they reached the stable door. Again he passed her the reins, watching closely as she led the mare in before removing her saddle and rubbing her down. He nodded his head, appraising her quick, competent movements with obvious if silent approval.

As she finished and gave Guinevere a final pat, he said briefly, ' Apart from the two hunters which you saw in the field, there is also my stallion, Hammond. You don't touch him, ever! And that's an order.'

Jane shivered, glancing at him swiftly. The tone of his voice was sufficient to deter even the bravest. Nodding her compliance, she waited as he continued with equal brevity.

' Some of the time you must help Mrs Tate in the farmhouse. This is the part which girls don't seem to care for.' His eyes glinted as Jane flushed, almost as if he was perfectly aware that she found housework tedious. After the slightest pause he added, apparently for her benefit, ' Mary Tate looks after my manager, Mark Fenwick. There is also another young lad who lives in the house along with two pre-college students.'

It sounded more like a hotel, Jane decided wryly, as Guinevere, in an abortive attempt to regain their attention, clattered her hooves against the stable door. As the noise subsided with a soothing word, Karl Grierson commented pleasantly, ' You'll be expected to help out wherever necessary on the estate, whether inside or out. So you might do well to think it over.' His eyes promised her that he was without mercy, belying the tolerant inflection in his voice. ' Most of us have to grab our opportunities, but just as long as you really need this job . . . you can come on a month's trial.'

He certainly didn't beat about the bush! Jane sniffed, rather inelegantly, as later in the evening she returned to her hotel. She was to start the following Monday, in two days' time. And he had left it at that abruptly, after leaving her with Mrs Dick. Mrs Dick had given her hot coffee and sandwiches which she had insisted

27

Jane ate in the study as the others were coming in for their supper, whatever that might mean. There hadn't been any sign of the manager or housekeeper, only faint sounds of talk and laughter from another part of the house. Then, after a short while, Mrs Dick appeared again with her husband, a rather silent man, who she said would take Jane to the station. Master's orders! Jane had been too surprised to protest. She hadn't imagined that Karl Grierson would have given her another thought once she was out of his sight.

She had still felt slightly dazed as John Dick drove her towards the station through the late summer twilight. As she had watched the setting sun streaking the clouds with scarlet and gold, and the water in the lake by the side of the road catching the colours and tossing them back to the sky, Jane remembered shivering convulsively as she noticed a lone pigeon winging its solitary way across the moors. A sudden, frightening premonition had swept her body, an uneasy foreboding of alien experiences to come. So strong had been the warning that she had had to force her thoughts elsewhere before she could surrender to the ridiculous notion that it might be better not to come back.

But there was no dismissing the fact that for the first time in her life she had met a man she could have reason to be afraid of. Insidiously her jubilation at having got the job was spiced with very definite misgivings. She knew instinctively that Karl Grierson would not have employed her if he had known about her wealthy father. And that she wouldn't last five minutes if he found out she had deceived him, even though she hadn't told an outright lie.

Taking herself firmly in hand, Jane sat down with a thump on her bed in the large expensive hotel. She wasn't used to considering a man's reactions, and she didn't intend to start now. Her hands shook slightly but she took no notice as she started to remove the pins from her odd-looking hat. She would have a bath, then phone George. She must give him time to replace her at the office, but she had no intention of disclosing her whereabouts. With their father in Canada, he would probably be too busy to think of asking. Apart from this, he might as well be the first to know that she didn't intend returning to the factory. That she had every intention of carrying out her long shelved plans, and that nothing he might say or do could make her change her mind and come home!

As she had expected, George was clearly furious when he heard her news. The roar of his voice echoed loudly over the line. For one defensive moment Jane held the receiver away from her throbbing ear until he subsided a little. She had been prepared for a certain amount of resistance, but not this!

'You've just got to be sensible, George,' she said quickly, as he paused for breath. Instinctively she knew that if she didn't go ahead this time she would never find the courage to do so again. 'You know I've never liked the factory much. I've wanted to escape ever since I left school.'

'Why didn't you, then?' George's roar grew louder, and he ignored or didn't hear the pleading now in Jane's soft voice.

'I tried, but a girl of seventeen doesn't stand much chance of asserting herself against a man like father.' Vainly she tried to hold on to her patience. Did all brothers have so little sympathy?

'But after three years! Surely you've got all that stupid riding school business out of your system?' Jane could almost feel the effort he was making to speak calmly. 'You're coming along nicely with the firm, and if you marry Felix . . .'

'I haven't the slightest intention of marrying Felix, or anyone else, as you very well know!' Jane clenched the hand which was holding the receiver, and thumped

29

her other one emphatically against the side of her leg. Exasperation almost choked her.

George's momentary flash of patience disappeared. 'You're crazy, completely crazy,' he exploded. 'Don't you think I've enough to cope with, without having to sort out your affairs? What am I supposed to tell the old man when he returns, I ask you? And if you imagine for one minute that he's going to set you up in a smart little riding school, then you'd better think again! '

'I don't.' Jane's tight fingers uncurled as she pushed back the heavy hair from her hot forehead.

'Then where are you going to get the cash?'

'Remember . . .?' Jane's voice came silky-soft. 'Grandma Browne's legacy. I'll have it when I'm twenty-one. It might not be a lot, but it could just be enough to start me off.'

'Then why, in heaven's name, don't you wait until you're twenty-one? It's only a few more months. Much more sensible to do that than rush off on some hare-brained scheme which might only end in disaster.'

Disaster! Dark shades of the premonition which had haunted her all afternoon. She shivered, fighting a rising apprehension. Trust George to look on the black side! But then he always had been a bit of a wet blanket. And she must remember that he was crafty as well as brainy. In those few months, which he referred to so glibly, they might have her married off to Felix. She might have little defence against their combined persuasions. It seemed improbable, and her fears could be exaggerated and groundless, but she was determined not to give them a chance.

She laughed, with a forced lightness, retorting smoothly, 'You're too pessimistic, George. Actually you've missed the whole point. Why should I risk my money when I get it? It seems essential that I make sure that I'm going to like living in the country, and can

30

stand the hard work. It's more than possible that you're right, and that I'll regret it, but this seems the only way to find out. You did say something about getting it out of my system.'

'Well . . .' There was a slight pause. 'Perhaps you're right.' He sounded faintly mollified. Jane knew the way his mind worked. He was beginning to think it would be wiser not to show too much opposition, especially when she was becoming a little more reasonable. If he gave her her head and played her along she would soon be fed up, and home within a week or two. His next words confirmed her suspicions.

'I'll do nothing about replacing you at the moment. You have a month's working holiday and come back. I think perhaps, we're both making mountains out of molehills. Just give me the address of the place you're going to and I'll keep in touch.'

'Oh, no. Not that!' Jane prayed silently. Aloud, she said quickly, 'It's an estate, on the Borders somewhere. I'm really not quite sure myself. But don't worry, I'll be all right.'

'The address, sister mine! I'm not interested in irrelevant details. You're being deliberately evasive. Apart from anything else, Felix will want to write.'

He was trying by devious ways to worm the information out of her. But he'd baited his hook with the wrong sort of worm. Felix! That just about summed him up. Frowning, she stared blindly at the receiver. If George knew where she was she wouldn't put it past him to turn up in the family Rolls and drag her home, and she certainly wasn't risking that!

Stubbornly she replied, 'I'd rather not say, if you don't mind. But I can assure you, George, if it will make you any happier, that my new boss is eminently respectable, and, I'm quite sure, will be as difficult to work for as either you or Father.'

A rather rash statement, but, as she ran upstairs a

31

few minutes later with George's angry protests still ringing in her ears, one which she was uneasily certain could be true.

George had lost his temper again and accused her of deliberately setting out to upset him. She could be up to anything for all he knew. Her behaviour, her secrecy as to her whereabouts was suspicious, to say the least! What people would say he didn't know! Jane had banged the receiver down in the middle of it, restraining her own quick temper with difficulty.

Now, as she sank down on her bed again, she was forced to admit George hadn't been altogether unreasonable. At the same time he had no right to treat her like a child! She felt a sting of anger when she thought of how he seemed to take it for granted that she would marry Felix. Indignation darkened her already mutinous face. Never before had she given her family cause for worry. Maybe it was time she did?

Coolly and deliberately she walked over to the dressing table and sat down on the furry padded stool, staring critically at herself in the elongated mirror. Frowning slightly, she passed slim, exploratory fingers across her smooth flushed cheeks. Her features were quite good. She had only been half aware of this before, but now, for some reason which she couldn't explain, she studied her face closely.

But even as she gazed, beneath wide, winged brows green eyes mocked at her own innocence. Unbidden came the reflection of a man's dark profile and, confused, her lashes dropped over beautifully modelled cheekbones. It seemed completely irrational that Karl Grierson could stir her imagination after one short meeting, when all she had received from him was a slice of lordly indifference.

Impatiently she shrugged, yet was unable to restrain a sudden quickening of her pulses, or stop her hands from undoing her tightly plaited hair so that it fell in a silken cloud, thick and heavy over her shoulders. Slowly she reached for her hairbrush and brushed it out, noting that it was full of gleaming lights as it lay tumbled about her slender neck.

Rather like a model in a French magazine! Curiously surprised, but with a complete lack of vanity, she wondered why she had never noticed before. Of course her maternal grandparents had been French. Not that she had ever known them, but she often wished she had. Her mother, she supposed, had been one of her father's rare departures from the conventional. He had met her in France during the last war, and, after a whirlwind romance, they had promptly married. Unfortunately, during that same war, her mother's parents had both been killed. Now there was just an assortment of distant cousins who never bothered to keep in touch.

Jane sighed, her smooth brow creasing. It seemed rather incredible that such a hard, north country businessman like her father could have married a gay, very feminine Frenchwoman. She herself must be quite a mixture. Perhaps George ought not to be surprised if occasionally she found it difficult to be completely conventional.

Inadvertently, it seemed, her thoughts flew back to Karl Grierson. Would he notice her appearance? she wondered. At High Linton she had presented herself as plainly as possible, but this image might be difficult to keep up. Only she had been almost certain, at the time, that her plainness had helped her to secure the job, and she shouldn't like him to change his mind.

Her brow still creased, she turned from the mirror with a tiny, almost imperceptible shrug. It was of little use worrying about this now. One way or another he probably wouldn't give her another thought. Just so long as she worked well. And, if nothing else, it would give her a chance of proving that she could hold down a job on her own, without the undoubted help of being

33

the " boss's " daughter.

Surprisingly Jane found that she had little time to worry. The weekend seemed to pass in a flash. Amongst other things she had to make arrangements for her car. When Karl Grierson had asked if she could drive, she had assured him that she could, but hadn't mentioned her car. Girls of slender means didn't normally have one! However, she was lucky. At the garage where it was waiting repairs, the proprietor said he would keep it for her, and she paid him several weeks' rent in advance. She had also had to rush out and buy some casual jeans and shirts, and some nylon overalls, which she might be expected to wear around the farmhouse. Altogether, with the hotel bill, it proved quite an expensive weekend!

Late on Sunday, as she arrived once more at the now familiar village station, Jane felt her former apprehension replaced by a sparkle of anticipation. Once off the train she dragged her larger suitcase down the platform towards the left luggage office. She would have to leave it here until she could arrange to have it collected later. It was too heavy to take on the bus.

In the office she inquired breathlessly how long she would have to wait, and was dismayed to learn that there was no bus on Sunday evenings, in fact very few buses on Sundays at all. To make matters worse the man behind the counter only smiled when she asked about a taxi.

' I'm sorry, miss, but we don't have one. Not enough demand, I'm afraid. During the week we do have a good bus service, of course.'

' Which isn't much help to me now,' Jane retorted crossly, her usually cheerful face flushed with annoyance. ' Mr Grierson didn't tell me about this when he told me what train to catch.'

' I don't suppose he would, miss,' the man grunted, as he walked around the counter to haul her case on to a shelf at the other end of the room. 'Would never occur to the likes of him to bother about how you were going to get there. Unless you were a guest, of course.'

'Unfortunately, I'm not,' Jane muttered tightly, as she signed the necessary chit before marching from the office with as much dignity as she could muster. Karl Grierson had a nerve! Or did he deliberately plan endurance tests? She wouldn't put it past him! It was a good job that she could remember the way.

Once away from the village and the shelter of the houses, Jane shivered in the chill wind which blew sharply from the distant hills. Stopping for a moment, she zipped her thin anorak closer around her slim body. Across the moors sheep roamed, cropping the scanty grass, the only sign of movement in the lonely landscape. Those hills, she supposed, away to the north would be the Cheviots, and the storm clouds gathering above them didn't look promising. If she didn't hurry she was going to get wet. A single star struggling bravely through the clouds sent her thoughts winging wistfully to her parents in Canada. She would have been wiser to have gone with them instead of dashing around here in the middle of the night! As she walked quickly on, Jane gloomily ignored the fact that it was only just after nine o'clock.

Then suddenly a scream of brakes on a sharp corner behind her shattered the silence, causing her to jump, startled, on to the grass verge as a car drew up by her side.

'Want a lift?' The car door opened, and the words, tossed casually by a friendly masculine voice, hung warmly on the night air.

To Jane, with still miles to go, they seemed the most welcome that she had heard in a long time. It might be all against the rules to accept a lift from a stranger on a lonely country road but, right at that moment, she couldn't care less. With a grateful, 'Yes, please,' she climbed in.

'Going far?' the voice asked as she flopped down beside him.

'Not as far as you are, I hope.' She grinned brightly at her own wit as she tried to close the badly fitting door.

He leant across her precariously and the car swerved wildly over the road as, with the ease of familiarity, he slammed the offending door, managing to stare at her intently as he did so. 'You still haven't answered my question?'

Jane could see the whiteness of his smile glinting through the darkness. 'I'm sorry,' she apologized hastily. 'I'm going to High Linton. But I suppose you know it?'

'Know it? I should do!' He sounded startled as he swung sharply back to Jane again, and once more the car veered alarmingly across the road. 'As a matter of fact I happen to be manager there. I'm just returning from a week's holiday. But perhaps you're on holiday yourself?'

'No, I'm not.' She blinked at his uncertainty as she clutched the edge of her seat. His swift appraisal and startling announcement confused her. Both Mrs Dick and Karl Grierson had mentioned a manager, but to meet him like this had caught her off guard. And while she clearly realized that she hadn't greatly impressed Karl Grierson, she had hoped to make a more favourable impression on his staff. Especially his manager. Only she had not been prepared to meet him like this! 'I saw Mr Grierson on Friday and I'm to come on a month's trial.'

'I see!' His foot jerked angrily on the accelerator, and she was startled to notice in the dim light the angry lines about his mouth and forehead. 'I might have known that Karl would make himself extra busy while I was away.'

36

The implied criticism in his thin, well bred voice was not lost on Jane who squirmed uncomfortably, hoping unhappily that she wasn't going to be the cause of any dissension between the two men. His tones.didn't indicate a very satisfactory relationship, but maybe he was tired and her imagination too active.

'I suppose I had to see someone,' she murmured, with the mistaken intention of pouring oil on troubled waters. 'In your absence, I don't suppose Mr Grierson had any alternative.'

His scornful laughter filled the car. 'You will find that Karl always has an alternative, if it suits him!' He skidded sharply around a narrow bend. 'Before I left I particularly remember telling him that I would see about another girl myself, but, as usual, he goes over my head.'

'Well, one poor Girl Friday can't matter all that much,' Jane pointed out diplomatically, considering it better to ignore his ill humour. In spite of herself the situation was beginning to intrigue her. It was becoming quite obvious that, for some reason or another, Karl Grierson and his manager were at loggerheads. Surely this must make for difficulties in the running of the estate? She felt a rising curiosity which she quickly suppressed, and, with pretended indifference, hid a delicate yawn behind slim fiingers. 'I really don't think we should be discussing Mr Grierson like this. After all, he is our employer . . .'

Surprisingly he took no offence. 'Don't worry,' he said airily, 'I'm not giving away any secrets. Discretion is my middle name. My first one, by the way, is Mark, and my last one Fenwick.' With a complete and bewildering change of mood he laughed gaily, his good humour apparently restored.

Jane, though somewhat perplexed, smiled obligingly. 'I'm Jane Browne,' she murmured, as he glanced at her inquiringly.

'And what would a girl like you be doing here?' he asked smoothly.

Her pulse jerked warningly. 'A girl must work for a living.' She tried to retort with matching smoothness.

'Which tells me exactly nothing.' His wits were sharper than she had thought. 'But if it's any comfort,' he went on, 'I can assure you that you certainly will work for your living at High Linton. Old Karl is lord of the manor, all right, and believes in everyone knowing it. He rules with the proverbial rod of iron!'

Uncertainly, Jane flinched, as much dismayed by the recurring note of bitterness in his voice as what he had just said. From what she could see of him Mark appeared to be a rather pleasant, if mixed up young man of about twenty-six. It seemed a pity that Karl Grierson's dominating personality was having such an adverse effect. Perhaps Mark just needed a little reassurance, someone to help him cope with his affliction, if he couldn't come to terms with it himself.

She said quickly, seeking uneasily to distract him, 'I don't really mind hard work, you know. Besides, what would I do with a lot of free time up here?' Around them bleak isolation pressed against the car windows, accentuated by mist and rising wind. 'Of course,' she went on, as his indicator flickered as he turned off the main road, 'you do have the Roman Wall and that sort of thing. I can always explore.'

If she had sought to divert him then she'd succeeded. He groaned. 'So long as you don't expect me to come with you! You might look down your neat little nose at me because I don't know what time Hadrian went to bed, but I'd rather take a girl to a discothèque than go digging in some Roman ruins.'

Jane giggled aloud. He looked so amusing. 'There's no accounting for taste,' she smiled. 'But a proper appreciation of the arts is something you should cultivate,' she tacked on with mock reproachfulness.

'I'd much rather cultivate someone like you,' he protested, cheerfully laughing with her.

But the laughter, fleeting as it was, died suddenly in Jane's throat as he pulled up abruptly outside the farmhouse. Too late she realized that the illuminating glow from the light at the end of the house shone revealingly on her face, and that Karl Grierson surprisingly happened to be standing beneath it gazing coldly down at her.

A sudden, irrational panic held her motionless. His bulky silhouette cut across the skyline and she sensed the hardness of his expression even while she could scarcely see it. He must have noticed her momentary amusement and construed it incorrectly.

His dark brows drawn together, he appeared to address them both, his eyes glinting. 'So you've decided to turn up at last,' he said caustically. 'I expected you yesterday, Mark. And you, Miss Browne, an hour ago.'

Jane stared. If it hadn't seemed so absurd he might almost have accused them of some deliberate conspiracy. She could sense his irritation held rigidly in check as he surveyed their confused faces. Why, she wondered, was he standing here anyway?

Beside her she felt Mark stiffen. 'I picked Jane up on the way here, old man.' Was his voice intentionally offensive? ' Seeing how you've arranged everything else so smartly, I wonder why you forgot to send someone to meet her?'

Karl Grierson jerked open the car door on Jane's side, his head bent only inches from her own as he eyed his manager grimly. 'You don't have to shout, Mark. Deafness is not yet one of my failings. You know damn well what I'm on about! Bill Clark had arranged to go home for his sister's wedding. I let him go, expecting you would be back. We're short-handed to start with, and your not turning up has meant a busy weekend for everybody!'

39

Jane sat, not daring to stir in her seat, as he breathed fire over her. His breath was actually warm on her cheek and, as his eyes slewed derisively to her face from Mark's, for one panic-stricken moment she thought she was about to be hauled physically from the car. Was it surprising that Mark was antagonistic if he made a habit of chastising him like this in front of other people?

Unconsciously she winced, her hands going involuntarily to her hot face, her nerves stretched taut. Some unknown part of her was reacting strangely to Karl Grierson's closeness. Certainly she hadn't been aware of any other man in quite the same way. Unable to account for a sharp antipathy, she stared woodenly down at her hands waiting for him to move so that she might get out.

Relief stirred actively within her as Mark broke the brittle silence. He said, a shade too defiantly, 'I don't know what all the fuss is about! There could have been extenuating circumstances.'

Karl cut him short curtly, his voice uncompromising. 'I didn't imagine you would return late without some excuse, but I just haven't time to listen at this hour. There are a few things, however, that we must discuss about the coming week. I suggest you go on to the Hall and I'll join you there after I take Miss Browne inside and make her known to Mary. I might as well finish the job while I'm busy.'

Bristling with silent indignation, Jane groped blindly for her smaller pieces of luggage as she scrambled from the car. Seemingly mollified, Mark waited until she banged the door before roaring off again into the night. Neither man had lifted a finger to help her!

Mortified, she followed Karl Grierson through the darkness, her fingers curling tightly on the leather handle of her case. 'I'm sure I could manage myself, thank you!'

His response alarmed her. 'Just shut up a minute, won't you!' Sharply derisive, he turned, reaching for her arm with a grip which hurt. 'You're a bit of an enigma, Miss Browne. I only hope I haven't made a mistake about you. For your own sake I hope not!' Coldly he propelled her across the road into the house.

He appeared to be in a foul temper. Resentment flared as Jane felt the strength of his bruising fingers. Once inside, fury vibrated helplessly through her body, and he returned her angry stare in good measure, his eyes narrowed darkly under the thick line of his brows.

Then her arm was dropped almost as forcefully as he had taken it when a slim, middle-aged woman came running down the hall.

'Good gracious, Mr Karl,' she exclaimed, 'what a fright you gave me! I was only out the back. I expected you back from the station long ago. Is this Miss Browne?' she asked, almost without pausing for breath.

As Karl Grierson nodded and introduced them shortly, Mary Tate looked curiously at Jane, whose own smile held a twist of relief. At first sight she liked Mary's homely face and soft blue eyes, which blended gently with her rather faded fair hair.

Karl regarded them both dispassionately. 'I'm sorry, Mary,' he said briefly, his eyes moving with warm affection to her face. 'I did start off to meet Miss Browne, but I got a flat tyre half way down the drive. I was on my way to pick up the Land-Rover when I found that she'd already arrived with Mark. They appeared to be having fun on your doorstep.'

His eyes sparkled with slight malice as his dark head inclined sardonically towards Jane again, and she almost gasped at the sheer injustice of his statement. She retorted indignantly, unable to stop herself, 'You know that's not true! He only gave me a lift. I had no idea who he was until he told me.'

41

The silence which followed her small outburst was brittle. Jane realized, unhappily too late, that it might have been wiser to have said nothing. But unfairness of any sort bothered her, and she was never too inclined to think before she spoke.

Karl Grierson shrugged indifferently, a clear indication that he was losing interest in the conversation. 'As you say . . .' He pushed an impatient hand across his forehead. 'I might only add that you seem to have got to know each other remarkably well in a matter of minutes, but apart from the bother it's caused, it's really no concern of mine.'

Ignoring her stare of mute protest, he turned back to Mrs Tate, his voice full of cool detachment. 'Our new girl appears to think we doubt her integrity, Mary. Perhaps you might explain to her when I'm gone that integrity is the one thing we rather insist on at High Linton.'

Quickly Jane looked away from those calculating grey eyes, feeling herself grow strangely cold, suddenly, overwhelmingly aware of her own deceit. Could he already be suspicious that she was only pretending to be as poor as a church mouse? With his quicksilver intuition he was just the sort of man to scent things out! In future she must be careful to guard her impulsive tongue.

She felt his eyes flick caustically over her startled face and flinched at the tremor that whipped through her body. Her breath caught painfully in her throat, making her realize that this man, with his arrogant good looks, might be very different from the boys she had known over the past few years. Danger was all very well for those who wanted it, but she didn't.

She heard him say, through the complexity of her thoughts, 'It would seem, Mary, that Miss Browne has lost her tongue. However, I must go, or Mark will be back to see where I've got to.' His eyes glinted as they rested once more on Jane. 'I'll see you in the office first thing tomorrow morning, Miss Browne, and I'll thank you not to be late.'

There was a silence as they watched him stride purposefully through the door, before Mary, with a sigh, suddenly seemed to collect herself. Turning quickly to Jane, she took her arm, guiding her into a large dining-room where the table was laid attractively with plates of salad and ham.

'I put some out for Mr Fenwick,' she explained, following the direction of Jane's glance. 'I rather expected he would arrive this evening when he didn't come yesterday, and he's always hungry. Now just be taking off your coat, dear, while I make some fresh coffee. Mr Fenwick will have his when he comes back, whenever that might be.'

The dining-room was a charming room, warm and bright, with a quietness which soothed Jane's taut nerves. She removed her coat, as Mary said, and walked slowly over to the fire. Above her head heavy old oak beams threw dark shadows across the ceiling, matching the huge oak dresser which stood against the wall. Attractive linen curtains in scarlet and blue were drawn cosily at the wide windows, and a low table by the fire was piled with magazines and library books. On top of one book lay Mary's knitting from which a long strand of wool hung down. A cat on the hearthrug yawned lazily and turned on her back, catching the wool with her sharp claws.

Mary, returning with the coffee, hastily snatched the wool out of reach with a gentle word of reproof. 'Georgina just can't resist something to play with,' she smiled, glancing sharply at Jane's pale face.

'Come and sit down, Jane, and have something to eat. Then you'll feel better. You don't mind if I call you Jane, do you? I'm Mary. We rarely stand on ceremony here.'

43

Jane returned Mary's bright smile, nodding her assent as she pulled out a chair. Mary went on,

'I'd stop worrying about this evening, if I were you. Mr Karl's bark is usually worse than his bite. I don't think for a moment that he intended to frighten you.' Carefully she passed Jane a cup of coffee.

Jane frowned, still wary, as she crumbled a roll between tense fingers, 'It was probably my own fault,' she replied. 'I shouldn't have accepted a lift from Mr Fenwick when I didn't know him. However, I do think Mr Grierson was rather unfair.'

Mary sipped her own coffee thoughtfully, her blue eyes reflective on Jane's hot face. 'Perhaps that was partly my fault,' she confessed ruefully. 'Mr Karl has been particularly busy this week. Mr. Fenwick has been away and lots of small things seem to have gone wrong. Then I did go on at him a bit about forgetting to send John Dick to meet you, and when he decided to go himself—well, you know what happened.'

'I think so . . .' Jane nodded doubtfully, her eyes still troubled. 'But surely none of this was Mr Fenwick's fault? Mr Grierson didn't even wait for an explanation!'

'Mr Fenwick probably didn't have one,' Mary retorted, so drily that Jane was left in no doubt as to where her loyalties lay.

'Never mind,' Mary smiled warmly again, as if she feared she had been too abrupt. 'We won't say anything more about it. In the morning you'll be going up to the Hall. Mr. Karl lives there, and has a secretary who comes in each day. He will explain exactly what you are to do.'

'He did tell me on Friday that I was to help you in the house.'

Mary's fair eyebrows lifted rather sceptically. 'He did? Well, I do have Mrs Dick, whom I believe you met on Friday. She comes in through the week but likes to be home with her family at weekends, and this is when I might need you. I'm afraid Mr Karl's definition of a Girl Friday is more of a general assistant for himself and his horses. Particularly for his horses while he's away.'

Jane drew a soft breath. This wasn't exactly what he had led her to believe on Friday. She spoke without stopping to think. 'He seemed rather fed up with his previous assistants.'

Mary's wry glance was suddenly cautious. 'We did have one girl for ten years, dear, but she left to get married. We've had one or two since. One had been well spoilt at home, I think. She was an only child, with wealthy parents, and never seemed to take the job seriously. I'm sure you'll be different, Jane. At least I hope so.'

'I will certainly try,' Jane smiled, but not very happily. 'Mr Grierson might be difficult to work for?'

'He's not very easy. But as long as you keep your mind on your work I don't think you'll hear him complain.'

Startled, Jane's eyes flew to the older woman's face, but Mary was already on her feet, making her way to the door. 'If you're quite finished, dear, I'll show you your room. I expect you're tired?'

There seemed nothing else for Jane to do but follow.

CHAPTER III

Next morning Jane was up just after seven and joined Mark Fenwick in the kitchen for an early cup of tea. If he had been ruffled by Karl Grierson's stringent remarks the evening before there was little sign of it on his smoothly handsome face.

'I always hate returning to work.' He grinned ruefully at Jane as she helped herself to a biscuit. 'I never could stand early mornings, not even when I was a kid.'

Jane stirred her tea thoughtfully. She wasn't all that fond of early mornings herself, but people did seem to get up earlier in the country. And after all, this was a farm. There would be a lot to do, and as he was manager, it must be part of Mark's job to see that it got done. Perhaps he should have been out an hour ago?

Almost as if he read her thoughts Mark sighed and added defensively, 'I've been out since six, so you needn't look so supercilious, young lady. So have others. You'd better get a move on yourself after this or dear Karl will be chasing you. And I don't mean romantically, darling.'

Mark apparently could be supercilious himself when he chose! A surge of irritation hastened Jane's footsteps as a little while later she walked along the drive to the Hall. He was obviously absurdly sensitive to criticism, and skilled in the art of gentle retaliation. With a sting in its tail!

Just as she was certain that Mary's few sagacious words after supper had conveyed a subtle warning, so, Jane was sure, had Mark's, if in a slightly different way. She had the message loud and clear. Her predecessors, poor girls, had allowed themselves to think too fondly of the master of High Linton. Arrogantly, but she supposed, quite legitimately, he had asked them to go. Dismissed them without another thought. Well, Mary need not worry that his new assistant's emotions would be so easily aroused. She had yet to meet a man who could make her heart beat faster and she couldn't imagine it happening now. One day perhaps, but not here in this wild corner of the country where men were too cold-blooded by far!

The drive curved suddenly through the trees and she came to the Hall—a long, beautifully built old manor house, designed, Mary had told her before she came out, by one Daniel Garrett in 1740 or thereabouts. In spite of her theory that it was people, not places, that count, Jane caught her breath. The house was lovely, graciously designed and mellowed with age. Lawns swept out in front of it like a lady's crinoline of soft green satin falling gently to a narrow stream which sparkled like a pair of silver shoes at its feet. A place to dream about, and dream in. It seemed marvellously in keeping that at the moment a lark should shrill high up in the heavens above her, its silvery notes mingling with the liquid ones of the wood-dove in a tree nearby. Reluctantly Jane tore her gaze away from the fascinating view. She had no time to stand and stare, much as she would have liked to. From one of those high windows Karl Grierson could be watching her loitering.

Leaving the drive, where it split as it curved to the front entrance, she walked around to the back. Here, in a warm, flagged courtyard, small, bright rock plants grew in the crannies of stone, and thyme crushed fragrantly beneath her feet. Exploring an unobtrusive corner, she found a door with the word OFFICE written boldly across it, and when she knocked she recognized Karl Grierson's deep voice immediately as he bade her come in.

Carefully, oddly hesitant, she turned the heavy iron knob. 'Good morning,' she said demurely, blinking con-

47

fusedly as the morning sun shone directly through a window into her eyes, momentarily blinding her as she stumbled inside.

'Wait a minute.' She heard him speak again even though she still couldn't see him. Only hazily was she aware of his dark shadow moving across the room until with a loud, short rasp he drew a curtain, effectively cutting out the glare. 'That's better, I think.' He spoke briefly, turning from the window. 'At certain times of the year the sun can be a bit of a nuisance at this end of the house. Come in, Jane. Please close the door and sit down.'

Silently she did as she was told, feeling irrationally that he had gained a few seconds' advantage. His office was larger than she had expected, and smartly furnished, but the chair he indicated was rough and hard, at the other side of his desk. It wouldn't encourage anyone to loiter, she thought, sitting down warily on the edge of it.

'You asked me to come,' she murmured awkwardly as he didn't speak, but sat twirling a pencil, gazing at her absently. Somehow Jane didn't think he was seeing her at all.

As if confirming her suspicions he gave a grunt, half of irritation, half tiredness. 'Yes, I'm quite aware of it, but I'm afraid I've had bad news this morning and I'm wondering what to do for the best.'

Bad news? With an effort Jane forced herself to stay calm. Surely it couldn't concern her? George couldn't possibly have discovered where she was already? Her green eyes clouded with apprehension, she stared anxiously into Karl Grierson's dark face.

His attention seemed suddenly to focus. 'You did say that you'd worked in an office? Your last job, I believe?'

'Yes.' Shakily she answered through stiff lips, her gaze dropping from his face. He hadn't been specific,

48

and while she hated his detached arrogance she didn't wish him to notice her resentment. He had the air of a man about to pronounce judgment and her breath caught nervously in her throat.

His next words brought a flood of relief, along with a curious anger that he had even unwittingly kept her in suspense when he might have told her straight away.

'It's Miss Cleaves, my secretary. I'm afraid she was rushed off to hospital early this morning for an emergency operation. Naturally I'm concerned about her, but at the same time I don't know how I'm going to manage here. She copes with most of the office work and there's quite a lot on an estate of this size. I'm wondering if you could help out?'

Dismay now obliterated all other emotions. If she was to help out as he asked she might well have stayed at home! The only reason she had come here in the first place was because it afforded a chance to work in the country, and to gain experience for her riding school.

'Surely,' his dark eyebrows moved noticeably upwards when she didn't immediately reply, 'you can't possibly object?'

Almost as if he had conferred an honour! He didn't contemplate that she might refuse. She looked at him with barely suppressed indignation glowing in her wide eyes. 'Since you put it that way, Mr Grierson, I can't, but I did get rather tired of office work. That's why I'm here.'

He regarded her with a faint impatience. 'Of course,' he agreed soothingly. 'But I don't think this need worry you unduly. It can be no worse than washing dishes for Mary, or cleaning out stables. It will only be temporary and you'll be free after lunch. Lydia should be back in a week or two.'

Taking her assent for granted, he glanced down momentarily at a pile of letters on his desk, picking one up and slitting it open with a fine, bone-handled

49

paper knife. As he assimilated the contents Jane watched him closely, aware of something within her stirring uneasily. There came an alien feeling of being out of her depth. She didn't want daily contact with this man—at least not in this way. It would have been enough to catch glimpses of him as she went about her various tasks on the estate. Alone together in this office there would be opportunity for him to ask all sorts of questions. Questions which might only be intended as the basis for a little polite conversation, but which in her case might prove dangerous. She knew instinctively that this man's mind worked faster than most, and that any small indiscretion on her part would be spotted and pounced on immediately!

His faint smile when he looked up confused her. Pink-cheeked, avoiding the dark grey eyes, she said quickly, 'I'm sorry about Miss Cleaves, Mr Grierson, but wouldn't you be better with a temp? Someone from a farm agency, perhaps?'

They looked at each other for a moment in silence, and it was Jane who glanced away first. His mouth tightened as he queried sarcastically, 'And why should I go to that expense if I already employ an experienced secretary?' He noted her deepening colour with an in-scrutable smile. 'You could be underestimating your-self. I'm sure you will cope. Much of the work is ele-mental, but if you find you can't manage—well, we'll say no more about it. But you must give it a try.'

Must! The word jarred strangely, but there seemed no alternative other than to do as he asked. To sur-render gracefully to the subtle imposition of his will over hers, as well as the indisputable fact, as he so tactfully pointed out, that he was paying her. 'Thank you,' she said with steely politeness.

'I'm not surprised you're annoyed with me,' he went on smoothly, strengthening her suspicion that he was playing her like a feeble fish on a hook. 'But it doesn't always do to have too much of one's own way.'

Jane flushed. He couldn't know that apart from her father's insistence that she went into the factory she had been used to having much of her own way. Was it surprising that she found it unusually disconcerting to be told outright what she must do? No one had ever ordered her around before, and Karl Grierson left her in little doubt that she must surely dance to his tune. If she intended to stay at High Linton!

Carefully hiding her hostility, she managed to smile demurely. ' As you say, Mr Grierson, I only hope you won't be disappointed.'

' Why should I be?' The curve of his wide mouth indicated that her remark was not to be taken seriously and did nothing to encourage Jane's intention to be polite. His eyes flicked her briefly. ' I advertised for a girl who would be willing to help out anywhere and, as such, I don't expect perfection. You might be interested to know, Jane, that your secretarial experience, if we can call it that, was relevant to your getting this job. I was aware that Lydia had a grumbling appendix and, apart from an operation, did need an occasional holiday and time off. By the time she returns I'm hoping that you'll be fairly conversant with the work here and able to step into her shoes should the need arise again. This is why I'm being rather insistent, as well as wasting a lot of the morning! '

Quickly, without waiting for a comment, he shot back his cuff, glancing sharply at the gold watch which was strapped to his strong, finely boned wrist. Involuntarily Jane's eyes followed his glance, seeing the fine dark hairs which covered his tanned brown skin. Like a kaleidoscope a dozen muddled emotions ran through her and she shivered as the finger of fate touched her lightly.

As he noticed, and applied the wrong construction, his eyes sharpened. ' If you come with me to the dining-

51

room, Jane, we'll have some breakfast. I don't suppose you've eaten yet. There's no need for you to tramp back to the farmhouse this morning. Tomorrow you needn't come until nine.'

Jane blinked, conscious of her faded jeans and top into which she'd hurriedly scrambled when she had tumbled out of bed two hours ago—an outfit which would have done nicely for the stables. She glanced at him uncertainly. ' Shouldn't I go back and tidy up a bit? I didn't expect to be staying.'

'Nonsense,' he said mildly as she rose to her feet. His eyes travelled slowly over her. 'You could perhaps take off that outsize jacket—and that hat,' he concluded decisively. 'Unless,' he grinned suddenly, 'you were born with it on!'

She could not fail to hear the mocking inflection in his voice, and her hand, incited by a small flame of anger, flew upwards, removing the offending hat from her head, uncovered the thick hair springing so vitally back from her smooth forehead had the sheen of polished copper.

For one startled moment Karl Grierson stared, his dark glance narrowed on her beautiful glinting hair. Grimly he noted the subtle change in her appearance along with the slight trace of defiance in her luminous green eyes. 'One might hope that you don't have a temper to match,' he murmured drily. 'Small wonder Mark was impressed.'

'Mark? You mean Mr Fenwick?' Stoically she ignored the implication of his words, but was unable to contain her curiosity.

He sounded mildly impatient. 'Mark, Mr Fenwick, whatever you like, is my manager. That is, I'm trying to shape him into one. I might even succeed, but he's easily diverted.'

Was that just a casual remark, or did it hold more than a hint of warning? Absurdly she was aware of a

52

growing sensitivity where Karl Grierson was concerned, which seemed rather silly, as they were still comparative strangers. Considering their slight acquaintance it seemed equally incongruous that he should be referring to Mark's susceptibility.

Her cheeks flamed beneath his steady regard and her small chin tilted. 'My acquaintance with Mr Fenwick being so brief, I couldn't possibly express an opinion.'

'Hmm . . .' His expression was remote, making it difficult for her to judge if he was angry. Decisively he turned and strode across to the door, indicating for Jane to follow. 'Actually,' he said, 'I didn't expect one. I was merely expressing my own.'

Jane's poise almost deserted her as she stared wryly at his broad back. He was too smart by far. However would she fare with this man if it came to a battle of wits? The thought of working in close proximity made her shudder. Fervently she prayed that the next week or two would quickly pass.

The office was at the back of the house but seemed quite separate from the main building. Karl Grierson led the way down long passages into a huge oak-floored hall. It was impressive because of its size, but at the same time it looked bare and neglected with only a few scattered rugs on the floor and odd pieces of good but wrongly placed furniture around the walls.

The small morning-room where breakfast was laid Jane thought attractive with its beautiful polished table and chairs. But here again the curtains and covers were shabby and the carpet threadbare. The whole place had an air of serenity and graciousness, and, while spotlessly clean, seemed to lack a woman's touch.

She gazed, puzzled, yet interested. Didn't Karl have a wife or someone to see to the domestic side of things? Her glance dropped to the table uncertainly. She hadn't realized that he might be married. He hadn't said and no one had told her, but it was quite possible. The table

53

was laid with two places. Surely no one other than a wife would be dining with him at this time of the day?

'Shouldn't we wait for Mrs Grierson to join us?' she asked, curiously disconcerted.

His brows rose as his hand went out to the bell. 'There is no Mrs Grierson,' he replied, meeting her eyes sardonically, as if aware of her confusion. 'A place is usually laid for Miss Cleaves. She leaves home early and has breakfast here.'

'Oh, I see.' Jane reddened, sitting down meekly as he absently pulled out a chair. Something nameless stirred through her veins. 'I only thought . . .'

'Well, don't,' he interrupted, dismissing her rather inane mumbling abruptly as he sat down opposite her. Speculatively he considered her pink face. 'If you're interested,' he drawled, tongue in cheek, 'I hope to marry one day, when I get around to it. But wives seem to demand a great deal of attention, which takes time. Something I always appear to be short of.'

Jane, recovering her equilibrium, smiled coolly, ignoring his sarcasm, refusing to take him seriously. 'Do you always put business before pleasure?' she asked. 'I have heard that a wife can sometimes be a help.'

'That, Jane Browne, is a matter of conjecture. There are other things in life besides matrimony. We aren't all romantics.'

She glanced at him and, as quickly, looked away again, an odd bewilderment sweeping over her. Of a sudden she was overwhelmingly conscious of him. A curious sensation of magnetism flooded her being while part of her mind warned her to go careful. He was distractingly male, handsome and assured, and while she felt that he deliberately teased her, she was not at all sure how she was expected to react?

Discreet reticence might be her best bet even though it was slightly foreign to her nature. 'I'm sure you must know best,' she said indifferently.

54

His housekeeper coming in with hot coffee and toast saved her the necessity of saying more.

In spite of the shabbiness of the furnishings, the meal itself left nothing to be desired. The coffee pot and cutlery was sparkling Georgian silver, the tablecloth and napkins beautifully laundered, and the bacon and eggs hot and perfectly cooked.

It had surprised her a little that Karl Grierson had joined her for breakfast, although she could see little of him behind the newspaper which he propped up against the coffee pot with a fine disregard for its antiquity. After assuring himself that she had everything she needed, she was left to ponder that it seemed slightly incongruous that he should be sharing a meal with his serving girl, or her modern equivalent Girl Friday. Was there really such a disregard for the conventions in this part of the country, or did her temporary role as secretary elevate her social status a little? Staring at the top of his dark head, just visible behind the newspaper, Jane felt sure that, given time, she would find out.

As the ensuing days went by she worked in the office each morning, returning to the farmhouse for lunch. The first morning she spent taking down letters which Karl dictated, doing his best, she could see, to control his impatience and adjust to her deliberately slow speeds. From there he proceeded to enlighten her about the general adminsitration of a busy estate office, some of which was quite fresh ground to her, but there was much that she was already familiar with. Before he went out for a couple of hours he told her how to get in touch with a firm of wholesalers about the late delivery of certain agricultural supplies. He also told her how to cope with the representatives of various firms when they called or rang. Those he would see and with whom she could make definite appointments, and others to whom he was definitely not at home! On top of this he asked her to make several business appointments, and to cancel one which he was unable to keep.

Working methodically but slowly, she managed to give the impression of average competence without appearing too bright. If by some strange, but not impossible, twist of fate Lydia did not return, Jane had no wish to be here indefinitely.

In fact Jane found the work surprisingly easy once she became conversant with the general layout of the office. Lydia Cleaves had left everything in tip-top order. Her filing system and up-to-date methods couldn't be faulted. Jane was full of admiration even though she didn't as yet know the girl, and she was forced to admit that the administration of a large estate, while interesting, was much more involved and complicated than she would ever have imagined. Indirectly, she supposed, the grounding she got here would, in a smaller way, stand her in good stead when she managed to get a place of her own.

Before lunch Karl Grierson returned, and after indicating briefly that he was satisfied asked her to come back in the morning. He also added some sketchy instructions about exercising the horses and told her that he would be away for the remainder of the day. He didn't say where.

Obviously dressed for town in a smartly cut suit, he dropped her off at the farmhouse door. ' Mark Fenwick will tell you anything you want to know.' He glanced at her sideways as he leant across to open her door. ' I'm sure that you'll be able to manage. Just don't try to ride my big black stallion when you go down to the stables. He would be quite beyond your strength, I'm afraid. And never say that I didn't warn you.'

The dryness of his voice brought a flush to her cheeks as she watched him drive off. She had no intention of riding his great black horse, but not because she couldn't manage him. She had yet to meet a horse she couldn't ride. Her indignation stemmed from the fact that Karl had seen her ride and must know her to be fairly competent. However, there would be plenty of work with the other horses, and in the office without bothering herself unnecessarily about anything else. He could rest assured that Hammond would be left unmolested.

Shrugging her slender shoulders, she turned quickly into the house. Mark Fenwick was in the dining-room drinking coffee with Mary, who jumped busily to her feet as Jane walked in through the door.

' I'll have your lunch on the table in a few minutes, dear,' she said smiling. ' We've just finished ours. I was rather worried about your breakfast until Mr Karl rang and told me what you were doing.'

Jane said swiftly, ' I had breakfast at the Hall. Mr. Grierson said it would be quicker than coming back here.'

' Of course, dear,' Mary agreed soberly, her blue eyes thoughtful as she picked up her empty cup. She added, ' We're all sorry about Lydia. When I rang the hospital about an hour ago they told me that she had had her operation and was comfortable. I was just saying to Mr Fenwick here that it's a good job you can manage until she gets better. It's really wonderful the way things have worked out, you being used to office work and that sort of thing. It'll be quite a load off Mr Karl's mind.'

Jane smiled. She didn't say that it was yet another of several peculiar coincidences which had happened since she had left home. Mary wouldn't understand, but fate had a strange habit of producing unexpected twists.

As Mary disappeared into the kitchen Jane realized that Mark hadn't spoken since she had come in. Now he turned to her moodily, his eyes bleak. ' I suppose Karl has gone down to the hospital? ' he muttered.

Jane glanced at him quickly. Although she had only

known him for a very short time he spoke with the familiarity of an old acquaintance. She wasn't quite sure how to take it. She replied carefully, 'If you mean Mr Grierson—well, he might have done. But actually he didn't say, and it was scarcely my business to ask.'

Mark stared at her sharply, the caricature of a sulky schoolboy. 'I do mean Mr Grierson,' he retorted with emphasis. 'And you needn't be so hoity-toity! I suppose you're all set to step into Lydia's shoes now that she's gone?'

Jane swung around to him, startled. 'Mark,' she answered, with equal sharpness, 'I have no intention of stepping into anyone's shoes, except, perhaps, those of my predecessors. The sooner Miss Cleaves returns, the better I shall be pleased.'

Her green eyes sparkling with irritation she turned and ran upstairs to wash her hands, not waiting for any further comment. Let him make what he likes of that, she thought scornfully as she ran warm water into the bathroom basin. But as the basin filled with water, so doubts began to fill her head. Blindly she stared into the mirror. Maybe she shouldn't have spoken so sharply? Perhaps as Mark was manager she should have adopted a more humble demeanour, but his own remarks were not what she would have expected from someone in his position. Doubtfully she frowned at her reflection, a sudden curiosity about Miss Cleaves stirring through her. She must indeed be very attractive to have both Mark and Karl Grierson obviously interested in her. Jane's frown deepened. Could Lydia be the reason for the antagonism which clearly existed between the two men? But if so, wouldn't it be easy for Karl to advise his manager to seek employment elsewhere?

Jane grimaced, hastily drying her hands on a snowy white towel. Conjecture wouldn't get her very far at this stage, not on her first day here. Time would undoubtedly make many things clear if she practised a little patience.

Downstairs again she discovered to her relief that Mark had gone, and she was left to eat her lunch in peaceful solitude. Taking her empty dishes into the kitchen after she had finished, she asked Mary if she could help with the washing-up before going out to the stables. The kitchen was another large room just off the dining-room, and crockery was piled high at the sink. Mary was busy baking girdle scones, obviously meant for tea, on a floury griddle.

She glanced around gratefully as Jane spoke, her face pink from the heat of the cooker. 'That would be nice, dear, although I do have a dishwasher. I can show you how to load it if you can wait until I finish here, then you'll know how to do it yourself another time.'

Jane looked with interest at the dishwasher. 'Actually Mary, I think I can manage. You just carry on with your baking. It's exactly the same make as the one we have at home . . .' She nodded as she saw the name on the side of the machine, and picked up the first batch of dishes.

'Our last girl scarcely knew how to wash dishes, let alone work a dishwasher,' Mary observed drily as she watched Jane working. She went on with gentle interest, 'How does your mother come to have one, dear? Does she have a large family?'

Hastily Jane bent over the machine. How did her mother come to have one? She supposed because she was usually able to afford every labour-saving device. Not because of a particularly large family, although she did entertain a lot. In business this seemed to be imperative, but she could scarcely tell Mary this. 'I don't really know,' she murmured evasively. 'I expect she just picked it up somewhere.'

'Yes, of course, dear.' Mary turned back to her stove, fortunately too busy to consider the ethics of Jane's reply. 'Everyone seems to have them nowadays.

They aren't a luxury any more. Usually,' she added, as she carefully turned her scones, 'Hilda Dick does the dishes before she goes home, but this afternoon she's had to go down to the dairy. Bill Clark—he's the student who has gone to his sister's wedding this weekend—generally works there, and it was to be your job this week. But then you can't manage that along with the office work and the stables. Those horses take up quite a bit of time.'

Hesitantly Jane said, 'I expect Miss Cleaves will soon be back? Mr Grierson seemed to think so, anyway.'

Mary sniffed, retorting sharply, 'She might if she hears about you!' Then she bit her lip, looking rather ashamed. 'I'm sorry, dear, that just slipped out. Take no notice. Lydia is very efficient, and I shouldn't have said that, especially as she's such an old friend of the family, so to speak.'

Jane frowned, puzzled as she glanced at Mary's vexed face. She wasn't aware that Mary had committed any great indiscretion. Naturally Lydia Cleaves might be worried about her job. With a bright smile she attempted to fill the uneasy silence. 'I was under the impression that Miss Cleaves was quite young?'

'Oh, yes, she is.' Mary's face cleared slowly. 'I didn't mean old in that sense. She's about twenty-six, the same age as Mr Fenwick. Not that that's relevant, but her father used to be farm manager here before Mr Fenwick came. When old Mr Grierson, Karl's father, was alive.'

'I see,' Jane replied tentatively as Mary paused. 'Then I expect it was convenient for Lydia to work here with her family?'

Mary appeared to consider this carefully. 'To begin with,' she frowned, 'I suppose it was. But then her father was killed in an accident on the estate. Afterwards her mother went to live with her sister in Hexham, and Lydia went with her.'

'So she has quite a way to travel each day?' Too late Jane remembered that Karl had told her this over breakfast.

'She does.' Mary glanced at her quickly, then averted her gaze. 'Old Mr Grierson felt responsible for the family, you see, and arranged for her to have a little car. Mind you,' she added firmly, 'Lydia really does work hard, and there's a lot to do, especially since Mr Karl started to run more of the estate himself.'

Jane nodded thoughtfully as she locked the door of the dishwasher before switching on the electricity. In spite of Mary's unstinted praise, her enthusiasm for Lydia didn't seem to ring true. Somewhere along the line there was something that Mary wasn't at all happy about. Something which worried her inwardly, like a recurring dream, without shadow or substance. 'I suppose,' Jane ventured cautiously, 'Mr Grierson and Miss Cleaves more or less grew up together?'

Mary wiped the heavy iron griddle with a piece of kitchen paper before putting it away. 'Mr Karl is almost ten years older than Lydia, dear, and was away at school and university. But Lydia's father was a very good manager and old Mr Grierson didn't believe in paying high salaries. I think, to begin with anyway, that Mr Karl felt he owed the family something. But I'm not at all sure what he thinks now.'

If at first Jane's own curiosity had been transitory she found it growing as the days went by. Looking back she was suddenly surprised to find that she had been at High Linton for more than a week, and already, in spite of being so busy, was beginning to settle down and enjoy her new life. The factory in Bradford might have been in another world. In small ways she missed her family, particularly her mother, but she found herself getting on wonderfully well without them. The sight of the windswept moors, the high rolling fells which topped the green wooded valleys could sweep all thoughts of them from her mind.

She did remember to ring George as she had prom-ised, from the bright red telephone box in the nearby village, only it wasn't George who answered this time, but his wife, Gail. Jane sighed. Gail was almost worse than George when it came to making a great ado about nothing! And while she did agree to give George a message, she rather coldly refused to promise that everything would be all right.

'I do think you're being very foolish, Jane,' her voice blended with the intermittent crackle on the line. 'You're placing us in a very awkward position. You could quite easily have waited until your parents came home, then looked for a job in this locality. I fail to think what your father's going to say when he re-turns . . .'

Jane replaced the receiver quickly at the three pips, pleading lack of change and pretending not to hear when Gail advised her to reverse the call. Gail obvi-ously had a lot more to say, but Jane guessed that it would be all along the same lines. Gail just didn't seem to realize that jobs like the one she had now weren't exactly two a penny. People were keen to em-ploy au pair girls to look after their children, but they rarely considered it necessary to have someone full-time to look after their horses. She had been fortunate to find such a job at High Linton, and meant to hang on to it.

She decided not to contact George or Gail again, but to wait until she could speak to her father. He would probably be too busy making his presence felt at the factory ever to bother about her departure. And by the time he fully realized she had gone he would be used to the idea.

It wasn't as if her work at High Linton was so very easy! She found Karl Grierson an exacting employer, although scrupulously fair. Mornings in the office were occasionally devastating but never dull. Generally his manner was sharply decisive, so much so that she was often surprised to note how gentle he could be when he spoke to Mary or his horses. Of course Mary had been his nurse when he was small, so there was bound to be a certain affection. She often wondered why Mary hadn't stayed on at the Hall as his housekeeper instead of slaving as she did at the farmhouse.

And there were other things which aroused Jane's lively curiosity. Why, she thought, did Karl spend so little on the Hall when, obviously, he was a wealthy man. He didn't seem to consider it as a home at all, just a place to eat and sleep in. Surely for him it must hold many happy associations? Then Mark too qualified for a question mark. In no way did he seem to fit into her idea of a competent farm manager. Karl seemed to advise and make decisions for him all the time, while Mark went out of his way to give the impression that he ran the estate almost single-handed. None of which seemed to add up so far as Jane could see.

However, as she told herself sternly one windy October morning as she sorted mail, none of this need concern her, and it wouldn't be a great disaster if she never knew any of the answers!

Karl Grierson appeared just as she was finishing. 'Good morning, Jane,' he said smoothly, a sharp note running through his voice, as he walked in through the doorway. 'You're late. I came in earlier, but you weren't here. However, I'll forgive you if you can assure me that you rang Brysons yesterday about that delivery of cattle compounds. If you remember, you were to ring them when I went out, but I've just been talking to John Dick and he tells me that it still hasn't arrived.'

'I'm sorry, Mr Grierson,' Jane frowned, gazing at him with a flicker of indignation in her wide green eyes.

'I did leave a memo on your desk, but you probably haven't seen it yet. The firm said, and I quote, that your order was definitely cancelled, and while they are quite willing to supply if you re-order, your previous order has now gone to someone else, and that particular commodity being in short supply, you would now have to wait a considerable time for delivery.'

'Miss Browne!' The terse thump of his fist on the top of her desk startled her, as did the darkening of his hard face. 'Didn't you damn well ask who had cancelled that order? How long ago, did they say?'

'About a week, I think.'

'You really should try to be clear about such matters, Miss Browne!' His voice cut sharply.

She looked at him with growing resentment, feeling the brunt of his displeasure. 'I can certainly ring and confirm it, Mr Grierson if you're not satisfied. I did try to find out who was responsible.'

'Lydia?' For one tense moment his eyes held hers disconcertingly.

'No. They said a gentleman, but could give no name.'

'We'll soon see about that!' His eyes narrowed angrily as they surveyed her grimly. 'Just get me the number, will you, and fast!'

Jane dialled with nervous fingers, and he took the receiver. 'Put me through to whoever's in charge,' he snapped.

With a murmured excuse, which he obviously didn't hear, Jane left her chair and walked to the window. It might seem foolish, but from the distance of a few yards she felt safer. The furious tones of Karl's deep voice echoed around the room. She shuddered. He could be quite brutal when he chose. She knew a swift compunction for the person on the other end of the line.

The receiver crashed, and he turned abruptly to look at her flushed face. 'I owe you an apology, Jane, I'm afraid,' he said curtly. 'The order was cancelled. By

64

one Mark Fenwick. I intend to have a word with that
young man! '

CHAPTER IV

Jane was taken completely by surprise. Surely there must be some mistake. So far as she knew Mark had never mentioned the order, and, although he did have an office in the farmhouse, most of the farm supplies were ordered from here. She walked back to her desk and sat down rather helplessly, while Karl Grierson's eyes glittered angrily over her.

'There could have been some misunderstanding,' she frowned. 'Didn't you discuss the order with him before it went out?'

'This particular order was not discussed.'

'But if he cancelled it he must have known about it?' She didn't realize as she spoke that her voice was oddly defensive. 'Perhaps your stockman mentioned it?'

'No.' He still sat on the corner of her desk. Too near for comfort, and his gaze sharpened slightly as he looked down at her. 'No, it wasn't John Dick. I think I know what happened, and it's nothing you can sort out. I've ordered another lot, as you no doubt heard, but it's damned inconvenient. It rather upsets an experimental project which John and I were hoping to complete.'

Jane's lashes fell on her smooth cheeks as she tried desperately to concentrate. If John Dick hadn't said anything then it must have been someone from this office. It could only be Lydia Cleaves. Perhaps inadvertently she had divulged the information? Was this why Karl looked suddenly despondent, tight-lipped and remote?

Painfully refusing to evaluate such thoughts, she said impulsively, 'Sometimes I think you ought to let Mark do more, take more responsibility. Two heads are often better than one. In fact this slight fiasco proves it. If he'd known how important this order was—well, this mistake might have been avoided.'

Wrongly timed, her advice was not well received. Karl
Grierson's face hardened coldly as his hand shot out to
grasp her wrist as it lay on the desk in front of her. His
fingers hurt, and as a small gasp of alarm escaped Jane's
lips she knew with dismay that his cruel grip reflected
a violence held rigidly under control. She thought, for
one startling moment, that he was going to shake her.

Her nerves shook and the blood pounded through her
veins as he lowered his dark head to within inches of
her own. 'Mark,' he ground out, his eyes boring into
hers, 'will have more responsibility when he proves he
can take it. Not because of your word in my ear, dear
Miss Browne! And if the way he's acting at the moment
is anything to go by, then I doubt if he'll ever reach that
stage. There are other lost causes without adding him to
to your list, as you'll no doubt find out.'

Jane grew hot and cold under his scrutiny which
lingered deliberately on her hot cheeks. Then suddenly
he released her and turned to walk to his own desk.
Flicking open a drawer, he pulled out a sheaf of papers
and returned to her side. 'We might try to check these
veterinary accounts, if you're quite ready,' he said.

For a few motionless seconds Jane stared down at the
dancing figures before her eyes. Her pulse still raced
disconcertingly, and she was aware of Karl as she had
never been before. She would have liked to close her
eyes and relive the sensation which had shot through
her body at his touch, ridiculous though it might seem,
considering the short time she had known him. Strength
drained out of her as she helplessly recognised an instant attraction. It might be purely physical, but the
strength of it was unnerving, something which she had
never experienced before, and which seemed to mock at
all her preconceived ideas of romance. She shuddered
convulsively, the tremor in her limbs bringing colour to
her cheeks along with incredulous disbelief. Deliberately

she concentrated on pulling herself together. It could only add to his anger, or change it to amusement should he guess the state of her emotions!

'Mr Brown's secretary rang yesterday,' she said, glancing at Karl briefly. 'She said there was a mistake about the number of visits charged for. She also pointed out that you've had sheep vaccine which she'd overlooked, but that, as one would almost certainly balance the other, she would put any slight discrepancy on to your next account. Or take it off, whichever way it worked out.'

Karl sighed, a deep, long-suffering sigh, which relegated all secretaries to unmentionable places, and the next half hour was spent checking each item on the closely written sheets. It wasn't until morning coffee arrived that Jane felt able to relax with a little of her old composure.

Even so, she felt too conscious of the speculative gleam in Karl's eyes as he slowly stirred brown sugar into his coffee. Momentarily he seemed a stranger, aloof, withdrawn. Then suddenly he looked up, catching her wary glance and holding it intently as he leant back in his chair. 'You seem to be settling down quite nicely,' he smiled slightly. 'What do your parents think of your new job? I presume you've told them about it?'

His voice was extremely dry, and Jane caught the sardonic glint in his smile as she looked away again. What could she say? What did he suspect? Yet surely it could be just a simple question? 'Of course,' she replied politely. 'But they're in Canada at the moment. Sometimes my father travels for his firm.' How easy it seemed to avoid the truth by merely twisting it a little.

One dark eyebrow flared. 'He gets around!'

'It rather depends what he's doing.' Jane grasped her coffee cup with nervous fingers, bracing herself for his next query which, surprisingly, didn't come.

Instead he said lightly, 'I was over in Canada a few

weeks ago myself.'

Carefully she pushed back strands of hair which spilled across her face. She still tied it tightly at her nape, but it didn't always stay there. She spoke without thought, as his eyes moved over her in slow deliberation. 'Mark must have managed very well while you were away.'

Immediately the words were out she regretted them. The smile around Karl's lips faded and his eyes were suddenly bleak.

'I must give you full marks for trying, Jane, but Mark doesn't need you to help fight his battles, which are partly imaginary in any case.' He watched her closely, the mocking twist of his mouth suggesting he could, if he wished, be cruel.

She gave him a swift imploring glance. 'I'm sorry. I wouldn't wish to interfere . . .'

'I should hope not!' With one little movement he rose to his feet, suavely sardonic. 'Mark must learn the hard way if he's determined to swim against the tide. He might find that there are easier ways of achieving his ends. And now, if you don't mind, Jane, I have other things to see to. I'll leave you to deal with the remainder of this morning's mail.'

That same day, after supper, Mark asked if he could have a word with her in his study. Surprised, Jane asked Mary to excuse her, and followed him along the passage, glancing at him curiously as he closed the study door.

'I'm in hot water with Karl again,' he announced without preamble, almost before his hand had left the door. 'It's about the order I cancelled,' he went on resentfully. 'I expect you've heard all about it, but I'd just like you to know that Lydia had nothing whatever to do with it.'

'Please, Mark . . .' He had insisted from the beginning that she called him Mark and, as each time she reverted to the more appropriate Mr Fenwick he objected, she found it easier to comply. Now her hesitation had nothing to do with his name. She stared at him, perplexed. 'I'm sure you're right,' she murmured at last, 'but I'd rather not discuss it, if you don't mind.'

'Well, I do!' With an odd note of defiance in his voice he walked across to the fire, moodily kicking the smouldering log with the toe of his shoe. Turning abruptly, he leant against the mantelshelf, returning her stare, almost accusingly. 'I know that we don't always see eye to eye, Jane, but the truth is that I'm very fond of Lydia. I do realize that you haven't met her yet, but you can take my word that she's a nice girl, and I wouldn't want her to lose her job. You see, through Mary, I've heard that you're very good in the office.'

So this was what he was worrying about! Not primarily Karl's order. 'Mary and I don't talk much about the office,' she frowned. 'How could she know about my efficiency?'

Mark shrugged indifferently. 'Through Karl, I expect. A habit carried over from childhood. He drops odd bits and pieces which she passes on at her discretion. But only that which she considers relevant. Nothing confidential ever passes that good lady's lips, I can assure you.'

Jane might have thought his last sentence complimentary if it hadn't been for the tone of his voice. Poor Mark, he seemed to carry a chip on his shoulder about everything and everyone! She moved uneasily. 'Surely you didn't bring me here just to tell me that? If Mr Grierson did say anything, his remark was probably purely incidental.'

'I'm sorry, Jane.' Mark glanced quickly at her frowning face, rather belatedly asking her to sit down. When she refused he wandered back to where she still stood beside the door, his light brown eyes suddenly appreciative as they slid over her. 'You probably think me

70

quite crazy,' he said ruefully. 'Sometimes I think I am myself when I allow Karl to rub me up the wrong way. But until Lydia makes up her mind as to which one of us she really wants, I don't think I'll ever be able to settle down and make a go of things.'

Jane froze with wide startled eyes, her voice restricted by a peculiar tautness in her throat. 'You mean—that Karl and Lydia . . .?' Confused, she was unable to go on.

'I just don't know.' Putting his own construction on Jane's few painfully uttered words, Mark turned restlessly back to the fire again. 'He's been very attentive since she's had this operation, taking her flowers and that sort of thing. I know I shouldn't be talking like this, but Karl seems to hold all the cards. What girl wouldn't fancy herself mistress of this little lot? You can't really blame Lydia if she falls for it. After all, she's only human, and, at times, Karl seems to give her every encouragement.'

Unhappily Jane looked away from him, down into the flickering heart of the fire. None knew better than she that there was some truth in his allegations. Hadn't she rung the florists twice on Karl's instructions, arranging to have flowers sent to the hospital. And the other afternoon, when he had left to go to the hospital himself, she had clearly seen the large box of chocolates under his arm. But in spite of Mark's brashness it might be cruel to tell him that she agreed with much that he said. 'Surely,' she glanced at him, smiling gently, 'if Lydia was in love with you she wouldn't think twice about anyone else. But even if she isn't, that doesn't necessarily mean that she's in love with someone else. She is Karl's secretary and naturally he feels solicitous when she's ill.'

Mark laughed mirthlessly. 'I don't follow, I'm afraid. It's not as if Lydia and I have just met. I'm sure Karl knows how I feel about her, and I think he deliberately lets her think that he is serious in order to frustrate me.

71

Lydia just doesn't seem to understand that she could get badly hurt. He promises with one hand and takes away with the other. Can you really blame me if I retaliate?'

'By cancelling his order for compounds with Brysons, I suppose?' Jane's softer mood fled.

He had the grace to look slightly ashamed, although he retorted defiantly, 'I actually think the girl in their office misunderstood me when I was cancelling an order for something else. It might have been partly my fault. I was in a hurry, to put it mildly, what with Lydia being away and being short-staffed. I probably picked up the wrong invoice by mistake. I told Karl that if Lydia had been around it would never have happened. Not that he was prepared to believe me, but he couldn't actually prove me a liar without making an awful fuss!'

Sceptically Jane stared at him. What exactly did he mean? Didn't he realize that many employers would not have accepted his explanation? He should be grateful for Karl's tolerance, and thankful that he hadn't been dismissed. Obviously he was waiting for a verbal pat on the back, but he couldn't possibly expect her to boost his already inflated self-esteem!

Coolly her eyes left his flushed face to glance at the clock in the corner. 'I'd better be going, I think, if you don't mind. I have quite a few things to see to.'

'I was wondering, Jane,' Mark spoke quickly, before she could move, 'if you would have dinner with me one evening. Just somewhere quiet, the two of us.'

Jane smiled resignedly. Mark was so transparent that, in a way, one couldn't help liking him. All he needed to do, she suspected, in spite of his advanced age, was to grow up a little. 'Do you really want to take me out?' she asked wryly, 'or are you trying to make Lydia jealous? It could be rather expensive. Why not wait a while and see how things go?'

Mark grinned suddenly as he gazed at her. 'You're

too intuitive, Jane darling. I must confess that was one of my reasons, but if you've ever looked in your mirror you must know that you're a very attractive girl. Even with your hair tied back the way it is.'

As her hand flew defensively to her silky head, Jane tried to frown disapprovingly. 'We could go out another time, perhaps. When we know each other better.' If, as he insinuated, Karl was deliberately frustrating him, then he was obviously in need of help. But this, she decided, must come in a more subtle form than that which he had in mind. She paused, her hand on the doorknob. 'If I were you, Mark, I'd try a bit harder. Pay a lot of attention to Lydia while she's in hospital, even if Mr Grierson seems always to be at her bedside. You can't be absolutely sure that he's the one she wants to see.' Without giving him time to reply she slipped quietly from the room, closing the door gently behind her.

Mark did look slightly happier, she thought, as she walked quickly back along the passage. If only she could be sure of the objectiveness of her own advice!

She still wasn't sure, weeks later, as she rode swiftly across the moors. The wind blew in her face, brisk and stinging from the north-west, deafening the sound of the horse's hooves thudding beneath her and the erratic beating of her wayward heart. She was up on Linton Lad, one of the hunters, following Karl up through the fertile pasture lands which cradled the houses. Past empty cornfields where golden stubble was rapidly giving way to the remorseless appetite of the plough. Blue and red tractors crawled, turning the gold into earthy brown straight ridged furrows, ready for the first hard frosts of winter, where wheat would lie, safely buried from the cold northern snow. Above the tractors seagulls whirled in screeching white clouds, searching for worms in the newly turned soil. Before nightfall they would return to the coast, many miles away.

Past these fields the horses galloped, Karl's huge black stallion, Hammond, leading the way. Up on to the fells which carried the hardy flocks of black-faced sheep, and herds of fat cattle. Grouse flew out beneath their feet, low-flying, settling again at a safer distance, while a majestic cock pheasant, well fed from a liberal supply of corn, strutted elegantly out of harm's way.

It was exhilarating to have the wind tugging at her hair, tangling the copper strands which escaped from the tightly pinned braids. Fresh colour drove wildly into Jane's cheeks and her lips parted in breathless satisfaction as she galloped on with careless ease.

'There's nowhere quite like this part of the country at this time of the year,' Karl remarked, reining in, in front of her on top of the rise. It was late afternoon and from this vantage point high up in the north Tyne valley the world spread out beneath them.

Jane nodded, her eyes dancing, but for a moment too breathless to speak. To the north the views were superb. Glimpses of the Roman Wall, Hadrian's country, right across to the Scottish Borders. To the south lay the Tyne, heavily wooded. Beautiful woodlands, direct descendant of forests of medieval times.

'Much of this countryside was not closely settled until the Middle Ages,' Karl said lightly. 'Hence the place-names ending in -ley, the old English leah, or forest clearing. There's Langley and Ridley west of Hexham. Then Slayley, Whitley, Broomley and others. If you happen to be interested?'

'I like local history, and I may well learn a little of yours while I'm here,' she replied demurely. 'I seem to remember our Queen coming to visit Hexham Abbey some time ago.'

'In the summer. The Abbey celebrates its thirteen hundredth anniversary this year, which is quite an age for any building. It was founded by St Wilfred, and, at the time, was said to be the finest building north of the Alps.'

'You obviously take a great interest in local history yourself.' She slanted him a flickering glance under thick lashes.

'Not particularly,' his lips quirked. 'I should take more. One can't live in a countryside like this without being aware of the past. We have our fair share of abbeys and castles. More ancient castles, I believe, than any other English county, with many old families still living in them. And, of course, we have huge piles of Roman fortifications. It always seems strange to me that many of the tourists who come here are only interested in these when there's so much else to see.'

'Possibly because of the publicity?' Jane suggested, following the line of the Wall on the horizon with her eyes. 'Even poets write about it, if I remember correctly.'

He quoted softly to her surprise,

'So they drained it long and crossways in the lavish
Roman style —
Still we find among the river-drift their flakes of
ancient tile,
And in drouthy middle August when bones of
meadows show,
We can trace the lines they followed sixteen hundred
years ago.

'Do you know your Kipling, Janey?' His eyes mocked her.

'Sort of.' Her lips curved upwards at the sides. 'I'm afraid I haven't read much poetry since I left school. I used to think some of his poems very romantic in a rather grand way. But then at seventeen one considers romance the in thing.'

He chuckled deep in his throat, causing the horses to prick their ears. 'So many years ago,' he teased, turning in his saddle to gaze at her tinted face intently. 'I wonder what has happened since to disillusion you so completely?'

She stirred uneasily, turning her head away, a shadow in her eyes. The light was dying a little. Soon it would be dark. Beneath his narrow regard she seemed to be moving in a dream. Lately she hadn't cared to examine the state of her emotions very closely, and she could have told him that it was the present, not the past, which she found most disturbing.

Instead she concentrated on the years between. 'I suppose I enjoyed the usual schoolgirl crushes,' she answered carelessly, bending forward to pat Linton Lad on his smooth white neck. He was rather a pet. Frisky, but obedient to her slightest command.

'It's rather a long time since you were a schoolgirl!' His tone suggested that she was being deliberately evasive.

Jane flushed, glancing at him too quickly. She didn't care for his insistence, putting it down to idle curiosity. There was no other explanation. He couldn't be really interested! 'I've had the usual number of boy-friends,' she retorted coolly.

'I can quite imagine you have.' His eyes, frankly taunting now, travelled over her. A slow deliberation, which sent unnerving prickles racing down her spine.

Aware, as she was, of his scrutiny but not his thoughts, Jane's colour deepened. Temper, which she swiftly suppressed, rose within her. Need he be so sarcastic? He couldn't expect her to confess that she had never been really in love. He would have no use for such inexperience, or patience with it! The Lydia Cleaves of this world would interest him more than she ever could. It was two weeks since Lydia had almost crawled back to the office, and Jane had seen how Karl hovered protectively over her. And how Lydia, with her blonde sophistication and provocative if rather silly mannerisms, seemed to accept and enjoy his tender commiserations.

Just as anger tightened her fingers on the reins he disconcerted her still further by asking abruptly, 'Where did you go to school?'

Confusion extorted the truth, as she glanced at him, startled. 'In Surrey. A boarding school . . .'

His eyebrows rose fractionally above his dark eyes. 'While your parents were abroad, I suppose. You have been around. I thought you lived in Bradford?'

'Not always.' Attempting to hide a growing distraction, she stared down at her saddle, uttering the first thing that came into her head.

'You've been pushed around a bit?' The brief kindness in his voice took her aback.

A muscle twitched in his cheek and warning lights flashed red. Jane took a deep breath. 'Not really. I've been well looked after.' Wary of his probing, she lifted her reins, preparing to go, only to find his hand on her arm checking the movement.

'You don't have to be ashamed of anything.' Now his voice held a hint of impatience. 'Plenty of people never have a settled home—or want one. Have you heard from your parents yet?'

'Not yet. No . . .' Only by keeping to monosyllables could she hope to retain a degree of truth without betraying herself or resorting to fabrication. Some part of her rebelled against more deception, and, when viewed in retrospect, it was such a silly, foolish deception!

She sensed his frown before she glanced up and saw it cutting sharply across his brow. 'Have you any family left in this country at all?' he asked curtly.

'My brother.' Slim and defiant, she sat very still, her face expressionless as he probed further.

'Where does he live—work? You've never mentioned him before?'

'You've never asked. He works in a factory.' George, like her father, almost lived there, too.

There came a sudden silence while the warmth of

his fingers began to penetrate. A pulse jerked in her throat, bringing a peculiar panic. 'I'm sorry,' she cried, wrenching her arm from his grasp with an effort, 'but I do have a brother and he lives in Bradford. I keep in touch and can assure you that he's eminently respectable!'

Her last words blew back to Karl on the wind as Linton Lad plunged wildly away from him across the fells. With a half smothered explanation he controlled his own horse, dug in his heels and followed.

Jane's horse didn't bolt. She had him under perfect control, but his head was turned for home and he went like the wind. She urged him on, clinging recklessly to his back, exultation and a nameless dread of the man behind her surging through her. It seemed imperative that she escaped him. She couldn't bear any more questions. He would never understand the pressures which had driven her here. Nor could he be expected to understand that here, for the first time in her life, she knew complete freedom. No explanation that she could give would sound convincing. It would be much easier to disappear when the time came than to try to measure up to Karl Grierson's standards!

Her thoughts whirling, Jane didn't see the hole in the rough grass when she came to it. Nor did her horse. His right foot went into it, and as he went down Jane flew clear of the stirrups, her natural reflexes saving her from injury as she tumbled on to the heather. She was on her feet in a flash before Karl could dismount, scrambling towards Linton Lad. Swiftly she grasped his reins, calming him with a few soothing words before running her hand gently down his leg.

Then Karl was at her side, his glance leaping swiftly from the startled horse to Jane. 'Are you all right?' Tersely his eyes clamped on her face, his own pale beneath the summer brown of his tan.

'Yes, I think so.' She hesitated, staring at him blankly,

78

clutching at her hat which seemed to be sitting on the back of her head. 'Just shaken, perhaps. But the horse, Karl? You'd better take a look at him.'

His eyes remained on hers a moment longer before he spoke to Linton Lad and bent to examine his foreleg. Carefully his sensitive fingers explored the bone while Jane waited, nervously apprehensive. She watched as he methodically took hold of the bridle and walked the horse a few paces. The animal limped, but only slightly.

'I don't think there's much wrong.' Karl turned his head briefly, his voice brittle. 'What the devil did you go off like that for? You might have broken your neck!'

He was all height and breadth and dark ill humour. Jane shivered suddenly, her eyes sliding away from him, the shock of her fall and the edge of his temper hitting her painfully. Not that she didn't deserve his sharp rebuke. All at once she was conscience-stricken. It seemed that she had deliberately used the horse to alleviate her own feelings.

'I'm sorry,' she said unsteadily, 'I really am.'

He frowned slightly as she drew a long quivering breath, her lips shaking. 'Stop that!' he spoke roughly, faintly exasperated. 'You've had a fright, but forget about it. Just stay quietly with Linton Lad while I go and get the horse-box. I think he'll be all right, but we'd better keep him off that leg until the vet's had a look at it. I'll be back in a few minutes.'

Silently she nodded, and his eyes spotted the faint bruise on her cheek where she had caught it on the hard turf. His voice sharpened. 'Are you sure you're not hurt? You came off quite a wallop.'

She turned her head to him, in control again, meeting his narrowed gaze with a cool level glance. 'Of course I'm all right. You'd better go.' Swiftly she lowered her eyes, not proof against a host of new

79

emotions which responded irrationally to the hint of concern in his. She clutched Linton Lad's bridle and stared down at the ground with fixed concentration. When she looked up again he was galloping away from her towards the Hall.

Hours later she sat restlessly in one of Mary's high, wing-backed chairs beside the fire. Outside the night was cold, but the farmhouse walls were thick, and the dining-room warm and cosy. It had been a long day and Jane was tired, but refused to admit that it was her mind, not her limbs, which refused to allow her to relax. Yet she was conscious of a certain peculiar despair.

Mary sat opposite, knitting, seemingly unaware of Jane's growing agitation. At ten the busy click of her needles slowed and she yawned sleepily behind her fingers. 'I must be getting old, dear!' She glanced with a half-smile at Jane as she started to fold away her work. 'I'll make a pot of tea, I think, then go to bed. Mr Fenwick won't be back until later. It's no good waiting up for him.'

Jane, glad of an excuse, jumped to her feet. 'I'll do that,' she said eagerly with a quick smile. 'You just sit still. I won't be a minute.'

In the kitchen she plugged in the kettle. A tray was already set with two cups and a small plate of home-made biscuits. She stared at it absently as she waited for the kettle to boil. The house was quiet. There was nothing to interrupt her thoughts. Mark was out, and the two students had gone to bed early. The evening before Jane had gone with them to a local dance which had gone on and on, and which, she supposed, partly accounted for her tiredness. Still, it had been fun. Mark, however, appeared inexhaustible. This evening he was taking Lydia Cleaves and her mother to a cocktail party. Lately he had been taking Lydia out quite a bit, although he still alternated between moods of optimism and black despondency. Jane didn't know if Lydia also went out with Karl, and since that night in his office, when Mark had confided his hopes and fears, Jane had managed ingeniously to avoid further discussion on that subject.

Was Karl interested in Lydia? Jane winced as steam began to trickle from the kettle. She found herself wondering about it a hundred times a day, yet unable to find an answer. Nor could she think why it should bother her so. But then she had never thought that she would miss working in an office, least of all Karl Grierson's! The knowledge of another girl working there endued a delicate kind of torture which she tried rather desperately to ignore. She still went back to the office occasionally, when Lydia was exhausted and needed help, but she did so reluctantly. As Mary said, Lydia would have been wiser to wait until she was stronger before returning to work, especially as they were managing quite well without her. This, Jane summarized, reading between the lines, was exactly why she had come back so quickly.

Jane shrugged impatiently as the kettle boiled. Carefully she poured the water into the warmed teapot, then picked up the tray and carried it though into the dining-room. 'I think I'll go and take a look at Linton Lad,' she said, placing the tray by Mary's side.

Mary picked up the teapot, glancing quickly at Jane's anxious face. 'You missed Mr Karl when he looked in before, but he did say that the horse was all right. And the vet has been here, so I don't think you need worry.'

The tea was too hot, and Jane drank too quickly. It hurt her mouth. Colour tinged her cheeks. 'I'm not exactly worrying,' she protested, frowning. 'I know he'll be all right. I just feel rather restless and responsible. Apart from that I think I could do with a breath of fresh air. Mr Grierson should be well out of the way by this time.'

Mary sipped her tea, still looking doubtful. 'Well, just as you like, dear, but I'm off to my bed. I think you'd be better off there, too.'

Jane smiled. 'Don't fuss, Mary. I won't be long, I promise.'

Mary sighed as she watched Jane walk towards the door. 'You horse-lovers are all the same. I may as well save my breath. But don't be long, that's a good girl. You do look tired.'

At this time of night only one light burnt at the end of the house. The farm buildings about it lay in almost total darkness. Jane walked carefully, feeling the night air cool against her skin after the heat of the fire. There was a promise of rain in the wind as autumn slowly approached winter and the northern sky darkened. She shivered as she stumbled on. In her haste she hadn't thought about a coat, but she hadn't far to go. The wind moaned through the wires along the roadside, a plaintive, lonely sound. Briefly a flicker of uneasiness overtook her. Impatiently she shrugged it off. She was tired and over-fanciful, but the dim light cast shadows, jumpy grotesque shadows, and she found herself unable to disregard a feeling of nervousness completely.

A sigh of relief escaped her tight throat as she reached the stables and quickly unlocked the door. Gropingly her fingers found the electric switch, flicking it down so that the building flooded with light. All was as it should be, the horses comfortable and settled for the night, but turning their heads curiously to see who had arrived.

As the light flared, Hammond called from the other side of the block, and the little mare Guinevere answered. 'Quiet, old girl.' Softly Jane closed the door as she spoke, before going over to the mare and giving her a sugar lump which she always carried. Guinevere took the sugar, champing loudly, nudging shamelessly

82

for more. Jane obliged, patting the satiny neck, then turned her attention to Linton Lad.

She moved to his stall at the other end of the stable, speaking to him gently before looking at his leg. He stood contentedly munching hay, his foreleg obviously not painful. Certainly he wasn't going to be lame. 'We are a couple of fools,' she chuckled aloud, running her eyes over him as she fished in her pocket for another lump of sugar. The horse responded to her soothing tones, bumping her playfully with his nose as he ate his titbit, regarding her steadily from unblinking brown eyes.

She stood for another few minutes beside him. Did he recall, she wondered, how they had waited together on the fell? How she had taken off her thin wool scarf and rubbed him down, trying to keep him warm as the afternoon temperature dropped rapidly? It hadn't proved very effective, but it had been something to do, and stopped her from worrying insanely about his leg. Karl hadn't been long, and together they had loaded him into the horse-box. The horse had even appeared to enjoy the fuss, as horses sometimes did. Only Jane had been aware of her growing distraction which she had been unable to discard. Not even when Karl, after a further examination of the bruised tendon, had again decided that there was little damage.

Jane sighed, turning away after giving the horses a final pat. Possibly she had been rather foolish to come to the stables at this time of night, but now that she had seen Linton Lad she did feel better. Then Hammond, the black stallion, called again, and Jane went tense, her nerves taut. Horses made good watchdogs. There was someone around. A vivid sensation of fear surged through her, blending with a strangely disconcerting shudder as the stable door jerked open, and she watched, wide-eyed with startled surprise, as Karl Grierson strode through it.

Her breath caught sharply as she stared at him. She had supposed that he was nicely out of the way back at the Hall. For the briefest of moments a little of her nervous uncertainty showed in the cool depth of her eyes. Why had he returned?

CHAPTER V

If Karl was aware of Jane's reactions to his sudden appearance he chose to take no notice. 'I thought it might be you,' he exclaimed, 'when I saw the light.' A slight smile flickered on his firm lips as his eyes narrowed on her startled face. 'Didn't Mary tell you the horse was all right?'

When he had called earlier she had been in her room, but Mary had told her. She blinked, uncomfortably conscious of his close regard. 'Yes, she did. She also said that you'd gone home.'

'I meant to, but then I had to go and see John Dick about a job which must be done first thing in the morning. I did intend to speak to Mark about it, but he was out.'

'I think he's out with Lydia.' Confused, she spoke without thinking, then held her breath, suddenly afraid, anticipating his anger. She felt the quickening beat of her heart as she moved slowly towards the doorway.

His dark brows lifted sardonically, but there was no sign that he was in any way annoyed. His gaze remained coolly on her hot face. 'Mark,' he shrugged, 'is usually out with someone. It might be more to his advantage if he stayed in occasionally.' He didn't mention Lydia at all.

Immediately, because she felt rather foolish, she retorted, 'You can't expect Mark to work all day without some form of relaxation in the evenings.'

'All work and no play, you imply!' His eyes taunted. 'Sometimes, Jane, I think you have me summed up as an absolute tyrant. I wonder what other conclusions you've arrived at about me?'

'Why, none . . .' Disconcerted, she dropped her lashes across her cheeks.

Noting her confusion, he spoke it seemed with deliberate intent, a hint of soft malice. 'I'm not above a little relaxation myself occasionally.'

As if she didn't know! She had seen how gentle he could be with Lydia! Scornfully her gaze flew to his again, yet she knew a surge of release as Linton Lad, obviously out to attract their attention, kicked loudly against the side of his box. She said hastily turning from the hard glitter of his eyes to glance at the horse, 'I came to look at his leg. I know he's all right, but I couldn't stop worrying. I can't bear to think of any animal in pain.'

Karl looked at her obliquely as he went over to the horse. 'So much anguish! Misdirected in this case, I might tell you. I wouldn't take any chances. Besides, horses cost money.'

Simple, concise statements. Ironically Jane wished she could share the same imperviousness, but she knew better than to attack him with words. The dangers of such a course had long since been apparent. Instead, she agreed soberly, 'I know,' and watched while he ran his sensitive hands over the horse before coming back to her side.

She said involuntarily, still looking at Linton Lad, 'I would like a riding school of my own, one day, but I can't afford to take chances either.'

'Such as . . .?' he invited lightly, almost indifferently. Yet his glance was sharper than she liked.

Silently she cursed her old impulsiveness. Apart from her family, she had never spoken to anyone seriously about her private ambitions, even though she had sometimes longed for a sympathetic ear. Well, she certainly wouldn't find one here! She laughed with forced amusement. 'With what small capital I have, I suppose. I might win the pools!'

She hadn't been mistaken about the sharpness. His eyebrows shot up. 'That is something quite different from what you implied. You talked as if you'd already won them but weren't prepared to risk the money.'

'I haven't,' she replied, too quickly, but quite truthfully. She didn't have her grandmother's money yet. 'I'm sorry if I gave you that impression. I could scarcely buy even the tail of a horse at the moment.'

His lips quirked. 'All young women who like horses dream of a riding school at some time or another.' He leant against a projecting piece of boarding by the door, surveying her keenly, coming to his own conclusions. 'You're extremely good with horses, but riding schools mean dedication. A lot of hard work without much reward.'

'There are different kinds of compensation.' The tiny mocking smile at the edge of his mouth annoyed her, awakening a curious animosity. Like her family he refused to take her seriously. Her eyes flashed wide with indignation. 'It's something I should enjoy, without considering the financial gains, which seem to be the sole objective in many people's lives! '

He grinned, openly derisive, his eyes glinting. 'Tut, tut, Miss Browne! I was just about to suggest that a nice husband with a small stable might be easier to manage. But he might find that sharp tongue of yours very discouraging.'

Now he was openly teasing, the mocking smile at his mouth blatantly contentious. Yet behind the smile he appeared to be studying her carefully. Desperately she sought for some kind of detachment, her eyes leaving his ambiguous face, slipping to his strong throat where his fine woollen shirt lay open at the neck. The hard smoothness of his skin, still with a summer tan, frankly indifferent to the weather, didn't have the desired effect. She felt slightly dizzy.

'Well?' he queried, unmoving as she stood tensely beside him. Darkness drifted outside the closed door, bringing with each new moment a deepening intimacy.

The warmth and quietness of the stables did nothing to arm Jane against the prevailing danger.

A nerve jerked in her throat as she attempted to keep her voice steady. 'I'm afraid I find the topic rather pointless, but, since you ask, I'd rather have the small stable. I'm not particularly interested in a husband.'

'Don't tell me that you're just interested in men?'

Deliberately obtrusive, lightly insulting, he quirked an eyebrow, forcing her to look at him again.

She answered quickly, refusing to be baited. 'It could be the other way around. Men might not be interested in me.' With a slightly shaking hand she swept the tousled hair back from her forehead, knowing a kind of helpless fury that he should be able to reduce her to such a state. Always before with a man, it was she who had been in charge of the situation. Not that there had been many men. A lot of boys, perhaps. Physically and mentally she had remained untouched. Even Felix's self-motivated siege had failed to make much impression. Why, then, did she have this imminent feeling of disaster? A definite feeling that Karl Grierson was going to be different, but not in any way pleasant!

He followed up her rather trite observation. 'I find that hard to believe. You must know that you're very attractive. A little juvenile in outlook, perhaps, but nothing which can't be remedied. Certainly not too young in years.' In the darkness his eyes slid over her, small warning lights gleaming in their depth, conveying subtly but clearly that he wasn't a boy to be dallied with and cast aside, should she have such aspirations. He saw right through her with those worldly eyes, aimed ruthlessly at shaking her youthful poise.

Her nerves quivered, yet she seemed unable to protest, as he appraised her openly. Her hair, tied in a casual ponytail, framing her face, gleaming copper-red in the half-light. Her eyes, slightly dilated, with cheeks flushed and softly parted lips. Their relationship seemed to have moved insiduously into a different dimension completely beyond her control. Thick lashes lowered as with an effort she sought to control an inner agitation, to remove from her immediate line of vision his darkly arrogant face. He was only seeking to antagonize!

'Perhaps it's my fault,' she tried to speak lightly, 'but we appear to be confusing the issue. I came to satisfy myself that Linton Lad was none the worse, not to subject myself to a personal interrogation. I think I'll go back now, if you'll kindly step to one side.'

The angle of her rounded chin. The slight arrogance, unconsciously reflecting a different status in some former way of life, didn't escape the man who stood in front of her. His hard mouth tightened imperceptibly. His expression was explosive although he spoke on a low key. 'And previously, I imagine, everyone has stood aside at your bidding?'

His eyes, spun glass, held hers magnetically, daring her to deny it. She flushed in guilty silence, not wishing to betray herself further. Maybe he was right in what he so sarcastically implied. Maybe such things were stamped on one indelibly, impossible to eradicate, but need he be so outrageously cynical?

'When I first came here,' he continued hardily, 'you were just a girl to look after the horses. Now, I'm not so sure.'

It was suddenly stiflingly warm in the stable, the easy movement of the horses blending with an occasional rustling in the straw, Of some small mouse, perhaps, that moved uneasily. The night wind from the moors moaned around the old roofing tiles, creeping into crannies, breathing beneath the door. A lonely, melancholy sound, isolating them completely within the thick stone walls.

Jane wasn't cold, but she shivered convulsively, dragging her defensive gaze from his with almost tangible effort. He wasn't serious—mildly derogatory, probably, but not in any way serious. Amusing himself for a few fleeting seconds, probing the depth of her assumed sophistication. At the same time, some instinct warned her that her limited experience in no way enabled her to cope with a man of his calibre. She would do well to tread warily. His suspicions might be easily dispersed if she treated the matter lightly.

Attempting an attitude of indifference, she tilted her chin even further. 'I'm afraid you must convince yourself that there is no mystery, if you choose to think of it that way. I merely saw your advertisement. I like horses, and I like working here. There's nothing mysterious in that!'

His dark ruthless face was intent upon her. 'Put it down, then, to a natural curiosity. You're a stranger, Janey, and not exactly a nondescript one at that. Apart from your looks, you do too many things too well.'

Her eyes dropped apprehensively to his hard mouth, and found it mocking. Again came the feeling that he was only amusing himself. Resentment changed her nervousness to cool hauteur. 'I don't think we need continue this silly discussion.'

He didn't reply. Nor, to her dismay, did he move. His bulk effectively blocked her escape route, making her virtually a prisoner with no means of evading him. Mutely protesting, she gazed at him, a little of her former bravado fading. But instead of stepping back he brought his hands up, clamping on her shoulders, his thumbs curving the fine bones. 'I think,' he said briefly, 'you're running away from a background that doesn't really count. Not in this day and age. I wouldn't want you to wear yourself out.'

Jane was not so much aware of his words as the jolt of her heart and the firm pressure of his fingers through the thin silk of her blouse. She caught his expression and thought it ruthless. She stared up at him blankly, her breath coming unevenly. She managed, rather wildly, ' I wish you wouldn't keep on so about that! '

His fingers relaxed and her muscles went slack as she thought he intended to release her. But subtly his mood changed. With deliberate intent he caught her face, twisting it up to his, his dark eyes glittering in the darkness. Slowly his hand slid from her neck down her long, slender back to her waist, drawing her against him until she could feel the hard strength of his body touching her own.

In that brief, electrical moment, her slim body pressed to his, her heart pounding, she heard his laughter, softly self-mocking. ' I seem to be breaking all the rules, Jane, but I find you wholly provocative. Or did you set out intentionally to tempt me? Whatever—I'm only a man. I'd be a fool to miss such an opportunity.'

Before anger surged uncontrollably his mouth came down on hers. Madly a throbbing awareness invaded each bone of her body as he kissed her. Her blood was on fire and shock stilled any further desire to escape. Nerves contracted as with a half audible exclamation he crushed her to him, pulling her slight body to his own, insidiously tightening the pressure until pain ran tempestuously with the fire in her veins. She had never been kissed like this before, and she guessed he knew it. Her response was instinctively of the senses as her hands moved helplessly to his shoulders and clung. She could feel every muscle in his hard body, every movement of his hands. His mouth, ruthless in its intent, drove every coherent thought from her mind, and the moment seemed to go on endlessly until he slowly lifted his head.

' That was quite something,' he drawled, his eyes piercing the gloom to her flushed face. ' You don't do too badly at all. One more thing at which you appear

91

to excel! '

A low cry of fury escaped Jane's bruised lips as she tried to pull away from him, her struggles futile against his superior strength. A pulse beat wildly at the base of her throat and her body went curiously inert. He seemed in no hurry to let her go, and, other than an half-strangled murmur of protest, she ceased to fight

There was a curious stillness about his movements, almost as if some unconscious force controlled his actions, and each small discovery, as his fingers touched her heavy curved eyelids, her pale, well boned face, an infinite surprise. Again his hand slipped down her back, exploring the deep hollow of her spine, until with gentle but irresistible pressure his fingers forced her pliant body to his, and his lips travelled sensitively across her smooth cheek before returning to her mouth.

If any moment could go on for ever, Jane thought this one might. She had no desire that it should ever end. There came a sudden sensation of whirling into space, spinning like a top into a void of burning darkness. Then, when all conscious thought seemed to be going, he was thrusting her away from him, grasping her none too gently by the arm, pushing her firmly through the stable door back into cold normality.

But for his automatic support she would have fallen. Her legs, deprived of their normal strength, felt rubbery. He didn't speak, and, as he turned to lock the door, she searched desperately through her numbed brain for a sufficiently annihilating comment, but none came.

As she heard the key turn with a decisive click she drew a deep breath, trying to steady her pulsing nerves. Emotion churned. Staring wide-eyed at the dark silhouette of his head, she wasn't sure whether she hated him or not. Instinctively she knew that his actions in the stable had been intentional. A form of punishment for some misdemeanour; she knew not what.

Through the darkness she heard him saying roughly, 'Come on, Jane. Home and bed for you. And until you can cope with this sort of thing, I shouldn't come back here at this time of night if I were you.'

Hot colour flamed as she stifled a gasp, stumbling blindly by his side. The harshness of his voice cancelled any former tenderness. That he should fling her lack of experience even verbally in her face seemed to be the last straw. Furiously she gathered her last remnants of pride. He had held her in his arms and somehow she didn't think he had pushed her away because he'd wanted to. She thought his expression a trifle too grim. Maybe he hadn't escaped unscathed any more than she had?

'I'd certainly not care to repeat that performance,' she flung at him bitterly. 'But not because I couldn't cope. I have been around!'

'No, you haven't,' he retorted, his voice hard and coolly perceptive. 'I might have enjoyed it better if you had, but at least inexperience is not without a certain attraction. Only don't try to fool me!'

'You beast!' she choked, anger and humiliation merging painfully. No one could ever hope to do that, she thought spitefully, but every nerve centre in her body rebelled against the knowledge that he assessed her limitations correctly. She tried to jerk her arm away from his steely grasp as they reached the farmhouse. 'Goodnight!' she whispered, as other words failed her.

He shrugged with obvious indifference as he released her, his eyes narowed beneath the light. 'You'll feel better in the morning,' he mocked, his taunting smile lingering in her mind's eye long after she had slammed the door behind her.

A week later Lydia Cleaves rang one morning early. Mary called Jane to the telephone just as she was finishing breakfast. A rather late breakfast as she had been out with the horses.

'Karl has gone to London for a couple of days,' Lydia informed her coolly. 'Before he went he suggested that you might come and keep an eye on things here if I wanted a day off, so that I might have a rest.'

Jane seethed, refusing to acknowledge a quiver of dismay which rippled through her. Irrationally she decided he had a nerve. If he had intended going to London it would have been courteous to have told her so himself. Apart from that, he must know that while he was away she would have plenty to do looking after the horses without having to help Lydia. Then there was Mary who had complained of feeling tired lately. She had hoped to find time to assist her more in the house, but apparently it was Miss Cleaves who was going to have the rest.

Lydia surveyed her anxiously when she appeared. 'You took your time,' she grumbled, morosely consulting her watch. 'I'm going to be late. I want to go to town.'

'Town?' Jane's eyebrows rose slightly as she walked into the office and began to remove her coat. She had been under the impression that Lydia was going home to rest.

'Newcastle.' Lydia didn't look up as she hastily stuffed papers into a briefcase. 'It's a chance while Karl is away. I'm thinner, I think, since I had my op. People often lose weight after a spell in hospital, and I need some new clothes. And I really must get something done about my hair!'

Jane glanced over her shoulder at her quickly as she hung up her coat. Lydia's wardrobe—what she had seen of it—seemed totally adequate. Jane hadn't noticed her wearing the same outfit twice. She said lightly, 'You have an appointment, of course?'

'An appointment?' For a moment Lydia looked bewildered. 'Oh, yes, my hair.' Tentatively she touched

94

her perfectly waved head. 'I'm considering a change of style.'

Something in her attitude suggested that this wasn't true. Jane frowned. Just what was Lydia up to? She needed a hair-do no more than she needed new clothes, and she hadn't been exactly specific about an appointment. She had a feeling that Lydia's sudden flight could add up to something quite different from what she had said.

'Mr Grierson didn't mention that he was going away,' she commented casually, as she sat down in the chair Lydia had vacated behind the smaller desk.

'It was unexpected—his going this morning, I mean. There was some business he should have seen to long ago, but he's been putting off. I don't know why—it's quite unlike him.' Shrugging, Lydia threw some notes down in front of Jane. 'You can start with that lot, and I've made out a list. You should be able to manage, but I'll look in, in the morning, to see if you're all right.'

'She shouldn't have gone while Mr Karl is away!' Mary sniffed disapprovingly when Jane returned late for lunch. 'Neither should Mr Fenwick, for that matter, although he does seem to have a legitimate excuse. But I'm not so sure!' Her pleasant face wore a worried frown. 'I'd better have a word with that young man when he gets back. It might be none of my business, but I would like to know why both he and Lydia had to be away today.'

Jane didn't say that she had wondered much the same thing herself, and felt even more curious next morning when Lydia informed her that she had decided against taking another day off, and wouldn't need her any more.

'I'd rather you didn't tell Karl that I wasn't here yesterday,' she said sharply, as Jane prepared to go back to the farm again. 'He did suggest I had a rest,

95

but he needn't know I took it.'

'I'm sure he wouldn't deduct it from your salary.' Jane retorted, disliking herself for the dig, but it was out before she could stop it. If Lydia had been having fun with Mark then she deserved a rap about it. It seemed that she could do no wrong in Karl's eyes. Why should she deliberately deceive him?

She wasn't surprised when Lydia flushed, a rather deep unbecoming scarlet. 'It wasn't what you think, Jane!' She stared at Jane's derisive face defiantly. 'There are many things you don't know about.'

'You could try being more explicit! I'm no thought-reader.'

It appeared, however, that Lydia had already decided that she had said enough. She shut up like a clam, retreating into herself with an aloofness which Jane, with her impulsive nature, found continually more exasperating. Getting to know Lydia was, at times, like associating with a brick wall!

Well, she was welcome to her little intrigues, if keeping two men dangling on a string could be so called. Intentionally or not, over the weeks, Lydia had left her in little doubt that Karl was just waiting for her to name the day. And, although Jane had never heard so much as a whisper from anyone else, she did remember that Mark had implied that Karl was more than a little interested in his secretary. It certainly couldn't be conducive to a very easy atmosphere when the two men worked virtually side by side. She found it increasingly perplexing that, as Mark seemed so unsatisfactory regarding work, as well as being a contender for Lydia's hand, Karl continued to employ him.

'Look, I might be in a position to do you a good turn one day,' Lydia muttered at last, staring down at her brightly painted nails. 'There's no need to jump so quickly to the wrong conclusions,' she tacked on with hauteur, aware of Jane's sceptical eyes.

'Okay,' Jane retorted briefly in her best office jargon. 'I'll oblige! But don't ever come to me for help if your plans become unstuck.'

Her advice, lightly given, rang a warning bell, as a few minutes later she walked back along the drive. Uneasily she remembered her brother using it regarding her own position, which, when she stopped to consider, might be much worse than Lydia's. Her father was home and getting restive. Mums had said so when she had been in touch a few days ago. She had begged Jane to return and talk things over, and had been extremely upset when Jane had refused. It would do her father no harm to practise a little patience! Jane refused to confess, even to herself, that she had no desire to go home, feeling a faint twinge of guilt because she rarely thought about it any more. Instead she had impressed on her anxious mother the importance of continuing her training, and that she couldn't possibly ask for time off as she had only been here a few weeks.

Secretly she couldn't think of any emergency which might justify her asking for time off, especially as she had allowed Karl to suppose that her parents were still abroad. Nor did she intend to devise one. Once home, her father would find some means of making her stay. He would probably have her walking up the aisle with Felix before she quite realized what was happening. Far-fetched as it might sound, the sheer weight of his personality was sometimes almost impossible to resist. Distance had always been her best defence.

Moodily, and not very happily, Jane glanced around her at the bleak countryside, the leafless trees which seemed to mock all the things she'd left unsaid. She could have told her mother that her heart wasn't really set on a riding school any more, that it was High Linton which she didn't want to leave, not just a place where she was getting experience. But how could she explain all this when she didn't really understand herself—not completely? She was only aware of a curious restlessness which was neither sensible or explainable.

It was over a week now since Linton Lad had hurt his leg, and still the incident remained fresh in her mind, refused to be dislodged. Against her will she found herself remembering how Karl Grierson had taken her in his arms. The subtle cruelty of his mouth haunted her dreams, yet throughout each day his cool indifference induced a certain warm resentment. That he regretted those few moments in the stables was clearly obvious by the way he kept his distance. But surely, Jane thought furiously, he didn't imagine that she attached any more importance to a few kises than he did? Her face burned with an inner humiliation. He didn't have to worry. She had the message loud and clear. He chose to ignore her, but she could have told him that it was ridiculous to go to such lengths to make sure that she was under no illusions. She was just his Girl Friday and, like the serfs of old, she knew her place.

Down at the stables she found Mark and was vaguely surprised. 'I thought you didn't care for horses?' Her eyebrows raised, she glanced at him carelessly as she turned to saddle Guinevere.

'I don't,' he grinned, standing back against the door watching her. 'But Karl expects me to exercise that great black monster, Hammond, while he's away, so I thought I'd better show my face.'

'You're rather scared of horses, aren't you, Mark?' This morning Jane didn't feel like being tactful.

Mark laughed, his fair face crinkling. 'We are in a nice mood this morning, aren't we! I wasn't aware that that I'm actually scared of horses, but perhaps you're right. I certainly don't care for that big black brute over there, if that's what you mean?'

Jane shook her head, her lips curling slightly as she tightened Guinevere's girth. 'Someone tipped you off—

98

or on—when you were a child. I know the story, and any psychologist worth his salt could explain it.' She turned her head, noting his downcast little boy expression impatiently. 'I guess I am in a bad mood this morning, Mark. Thanks to you and Miss Cleaves. I had too much to do yesterday. I react badly when I'm tired.'

'You can say that again!' He came closer. 'You weren't referring to Lydia and me sort of collectively, were you?'

Jane raised her eyebrows questioningly, her eyes mocking. 'Should I?'

Mark went red, staring at Jane warily. 'Is it any use my pretending I don't know what you're talking about?'

'I shouldn't think so. Occasionally my intuition works overtime.'

'You can say that again!'

'Stop repeating yourself, Mark, I find it irritating. You might like to know if only for future reference that I'm an expert at putting two and two together. But then you seem to enjoy walking a tightrope.'

His flush faded, replaced by an uneasy frown. 'Do you always talk in riddles? You could try explaining yourself.'

She retorted tartly, as she skilfully inserted Guinevere's bit, 'You might have to do just that yourself when Karl returns.'

He grinned sharply. 'So you contend that while the cat's away, the mice shouldn't play. Is that it, Miss Nosey Parker?'

'Cats, mice, and nosey parkers! You are being original this morning, Mr Fenwick. I'm only flashing amber lights. The rest is up to you.'

'Point taken. Okay, Jane darling, you win.' Mark subsided, suddenly subdued. 'I might only add that there are a lot of things which you don't understand.'

' If anyone tells me that again today, I'll scream! '

' Seriously, Jane, if something doesn't work out soon, I'll join you.' He gazed indifferently across the yard to where Hammond stamped impatiently in his box. 'I confess that Lydia and I were out together yesterday, but it was on legitimate business.'

So her suspicions hadn't been unfounded. Jane glanced at him sideways, unable to hide a flicker of puzzled disapproval. 'And Karl is not to know? '

' I hope not! ' He reverted to a forced lightness.

' You were buying him a birthday present. It's to be a great surprise! '

' Jane! ' Indignantly he stepped towards her, towering above her. ' What on earth's got into you? '

' I don't know, Mark. I'm sorry.' Suddenly it was Jane's turn to subside. Her head glinted as she laid it heavily against the little mare's side. ' Perhaps I really did do too much yesterday. Or perhaps it's just a strange feeling I have that we're both a bit out of our depth? '

He looked at her unhappily. ' I'm both out of my depth and my own worst enemy, Jane. It's a strange mixture.' His glance sharpened, fastening suddenly on her face as she bit her bottom lip nervously between even white teeth. ' You're a bit of a mystery yourself, are you not? Lately a few people around here have been asking who you are, and where you come from.'

Jane sighed, releasing her tortured lip. One more straw! She supposed it was inevitable. She rode up on the fells. She drove Mary down to the village shop, and went often herself on various messages. She hadn't noticed anyone looking, but she was around quite a bit. ' Who notices? ' she asked carefully.

' Oh, the local people. And those who walk the Wall, glad that our Roman conquerors are no longer there to impede them. Nero fiddles while Rome burns.' Mark laughed drily at his own idiocy. ' I don't imagine that our average visitor spares a thought for that half frozen army of legionaries who kept us safe from the wild hordes to the north. No! They walk the Wall, explore the digs, then wander down to the nearest pub for a drink and a good meal, and ask who the goddess is with the flaming red hair who rides the great black charger. Cleopatra? Or is it the beautiful wife of some long-dead Caesar who comes to haunt them?'

'How did you know? Or rather, who told you?' Jane's head came up. She stared at him, startled, too apprehensive to appreciate the picture he painted.

'Aha!' Smirking, Mark waved an airy finger. 'If dear Karl were to find out you'd be in for the high jump, my girl. He specifically told you not to ride Hammond.'

'He was restless, so I took him out. When Karl is away no one else seems to bother,' she added pointedly.

'Fine, then,' Mark grinned blandly. 'I might even let you take him out again today, providing you keep quiet about Lydia and me.'

Jane said furiously, 'I don't make bargains—not that sort!'

'You'd better make this an exception, my pet.' Mark exuded confidence of a sudden. 'My silence for yours, and no questions asked?'

'You pig!' Jane exploded softly, her eyes flashing. Yet nothing in this world had been like riding Hammond. He was a perfect joy to ride, moving with precision, never putting a foot wrong. And, for a promise, Mark would hand him over completely! Underneath, she felt a pagan surge of jubilation which faded as quickly when she visualized Karl's anger. She would be guilty of two offences; riding Hammond, and disobeying orders! She had no intention of telling Karl that his secretary and manager had spent a day together while he was in London, but Mark didn't know this. Obviously he had no idea that she had already promised

101

Lydia much the same thing. He seemed under the impression that as soon as Karl returned, she would relate the whole story. However, the price of Mark's silence might buy her a few more weeks at High Linton. The thought of being told to leave was more than she could bear. After today she must never ride Hammond again. She made a mental promise to herself—and Karl.

She also promised verbally to Mark that her lips were sealed. 'I should have more sense,' she grinned ruefully. 'But I can't resist him.' She meant the horse, of course, and wondered why Mark's brown eyes were suddenly full of speculation.

'A start for your riding school,' Karl Grierson said lightly, tossing Jane a small parcel after giving Mary a larger one, and passing another with a slight smile to Hilda Dick.

He had just arrived home that morning and his presence seemed to dominate even the big farmhouse kitchen. Jane's eyes dropped from his to stare mutely at the neat brown package in her hands, unconsciously noting its size, holding it warily, not quite sure what to do with it.

Quickly she glanced at the delighted faces of the two older women, then back to her own gift again, wholly bewildered. His words seemed to hold a double meaning, of what she was not sure. Her heart beat unevenly. Yet couldn't she be attaching too much importance to a casual gesture? A small peace-offering, no doubt, for his indifferent treatment over the past week. Or more probably just something which he had purchased along with his other presents, with no special significance whatsoever.

Carefully, as he appeared to be waiting expectantly, Jane started to remove the wrapping. Nervously aware of his regard she tried not to fumble, taking care lest what the parcel contained was in some way breakable.

Then, as the last piece of tissue fell away, she found a horse—a miniature, delicately complete in every detail. With started delight she gazed at the beautifully modelled head and limbs. A superb black stallion, an exact replica of Hammond, even to the flowing mane and tail, in jade.

'You've loved him since the first time you saw him,' Karl observed, watching her expressive face, the flush of excitement on her cheeks. 'I thought you would like it.'

'Yes, yes, I do! I do see the likeness.' Involuntarily a thrill of pleasure ran through her, mingling with an almost physical stab of dismay. She could swear that the little horse was made of jade. Her mother had a few pieces, all valuable. She liked to caress one piece which was small enough to fit into her hand, to rub it between her finger and thumb. She said it talked to her. She also said that a sure test for jade was to try and scratch it with a knife-blade or saw. If it scratched, it wasn't the real thing. There was something very satisfying in feeling a good piece of old jade, and Jane was almost certain that she was holding such a piece in her hands. 'It must have cost quite a bit . . .' she murmured awkwardly.

A small difficult silence was broken harshly by the demanding ring of the telephone from the hall. Mary, eloquently delighted with a huge box of chocolates, excused herself briefly as she ran to answer it. Hilda Dick, equaly thrilled with a slightly smaller box, put hers quickly into the bag in which she carried her house-shoes, and reached for a white overall.

'If you've any time to spare this afternoon, Jane,' she said as she went out, 'I'd be very glad of a hand in the dairy.'

'Bill Clark's long weekend again,' Jane explained automatically, nodding abstractedly in Hilda's direction, her eyes still glued to the small, perfect statue in her hands.

'Jane!' As Hilda somewhat noisily closed the door, Karl gave the girl all his attention, his gaze quizzical. 'Have you never learnt to accept a present gracefully?'

'Gratefully, you mean?'

Just for a moment his dark brows drew together and his firm mouth tightened. 'Sometimes, Jane,' he drawled laconically, 'I could shake you. You might, on other occasions, receive gifts from other men. It's not particularly ladylike to refer to their cost.'

She flushed with a flare of anger, which he aroused so easily. He knew, as well as she did, that the small jade horse wasn't the sort of present that an employer would normally give to his Girl Friday. Why, then, had he chosen to embarrass her in this way? He didn't have to give her anything at all. She took a deep breath, her long lashes flickering. 'I don't know that I can accept it. You must think what you will, but it wasn't necessary.'

He sighed, quite audibly, sitting down heavily on the side of the large kitchen table, regarding her patiently as she stood in front of him apprehensively clutching his gift. 'Presents, my dear Jane, are very rarely strictly necessary, but I usually like to bring back a few odds and ends, It boosts my ego to acknowledge the expressions of delight on the faces of the recipients. I shouldn't care for it at all if you were cross! Apart from that, you choose a fine way to welcome a man back from his travels.'

'Four days could scarcely be referred to as such!' she retorted hotly, refusing to go along with his light-hearted raillery.

'Tut, tut,' he grinned, now openly teasing as his dark eyes met and held her green ones. 'I've been as far as London. Wait until I go abroad, then I'll really bring you something.'

'But I don't want anything!' Strung up, nerves tense,

Jane thrust the little horse hard into his hands, her own trembling. 'You'd better have this back. I couldn't possibly take it.'

CHAPTER VI

Jane!' Like a flash his fingers closed over the jade
horse, while his other hand, with lightning dexterity,
clamped steel-like on to her wrist, his dark eyes brittle
on her flushed face as he jerked her to him. 'It seems
to me that your education has, in some way, been sadly
lacking in those little back alleys of yours.' His voice
was cool, deliberately insulting. 'Perhaps we could
start again. You're young enough to learn. To begin
with you can take this, and try to say thank you nicely.'

Rather desperately she tried to pull away, wishing
fervently that she had had the sense to say that in the
first place. Why on earth hadn't she had the wit to
accept his gift as a piece of cheap reproduction, instead
of making an issue out of it? But his words stung, in
spite of the fact that they were clearly based on the
impression she had purposefully contrived to give him.
Wordlessly she shook her head defiantly, her gaze
averted.

His eyes, taut on her face, noted her paler colour
and relented. 'Forget it, Janey.' The glint in his eye
was replaced by something less menacing, and his
fingers relaxed their hold slightly. 'The back street
image doesn't count. It's my guess that your life hasn't
been exactly strewn with presents, hence the confusion.
And since you've grown up some of the gifts you've
been offered probably had strings attached—apart from
that which they were tied up with.'

Catching the thread of irony in his voice, Jane went
cold all over. What sort of a life did he imagine she
had led before coming here? The satire in his eyes
suggested many things, none of which she cared for.
His gaze was full on her and she could feel the tension.
The picture he had fixed in his mind was obviously of

someone who had fought her way up from very humble beginnings. An alley-cat aspiring to be a fine lady! She had a feeling that her rejection of his gift had stung, and that, ridiculous as it might seem, his smoothly worded insult had been intentional—a subtle form of reprisal that she had dared to defy him.

Perhaps, Jane seethed inwardly, and somewhat childishly, it would be craftier to pretend she was full of remorse. One day she might find a way to make him eat his words, but, in the meantime, how much wiser to wallow in his sympathy than to drown in his anger! With a sharp little indrawn breath she said softly, 'You could be right . . . You usually are.'

'I thought you'd come round to my way of thinking eventually.' With that ambiguous remark he moved on to the floor, placing the little horse carefully behind him on the table. His eyes looking rather lazily down on her explored her warmly tinted face, and she felt the quick beat of her heart, a sense of strange excitement, completely unexplainable. Slowly he released her wrist, but before she could move his two hands went up to cup her face, and for a long moment stayed there. She made a jerky little movement away from him, but his lean hands slipped down to her smooth nape, his thumbs gently caressing the soft hollows of her throat.

Her curved mouth softened and quivered, and she was aware with all her senses of the magnetic strength which made it impossible for her to move or speak. Her eyelids flickered and fell. It took her breath away, the suddenness of his action, the traitorous response of her pulses to the warmth and pressure of his fingers on her bare skin. There came a sharp clatter from the hall and Jane's breath caught as her eyes flew open and met his gaze. Panic lent her strength as she jerked away. She backed away from him and saw the glint of his white teeth as he smiled.

She choked, ' Your arrogance is beyond belief! You're

a fine one to talk of strings! '

Infuriatingly he threw back his head and laughed. 'Next time I'll try putting you across my knee, you might enjoy that better.' But the laughter didn't quite reach his eyes and his voice sounded curt. 'I wonder just how innocent you are, Miss Browne? Perhaps one day I might try to find out! '

'Oh! ' she gasped, her cheeks burning. Then turning blindly she ran from the kitchen, and, when she reached her bedroom, flung herself across the bed. 'How dared he! ' she gasped again, aloud, as she beat her pillow in fury. She wanted nothing more than to be able to hit him, to hurt him as he was beginning to hurt her, cruelly. How could one hate a man and long to be in his arms at the same time? The memory of his hard mouth brought panic, and the thought of it against her own swept away all sense of restraint. Helplessly she remembered her own passionate yielding to the unmerciful exploration of his hands. His ruthlessness had stripped away all her former preconceived ideas of romance, leaving her utterly devastated, and with a hungry yearning within her such as she had never known before.

Wretchedly she scrambled off the bed, remembering the time, trying not to think, a mood of defiance following closely that of despair. Perhaps some of this was her own fault. Something about her—she knew not what—seemed to antagonize him easily. In future she must keep out of his way, if only for her own peace of mind.

Fiercely she grabbed her hairbrush, sweeping it through her long, gleaming hair before tying it back with a ribbon and jamming on her old cotton hat. Studiously she avoided looking at her face in the mirror. Outside the November afternoon was darkening fast beneath a leaden sky and thick gathering fog. Raindrops, swollen and translucent, fell against the panes, hitting the glass sharply, the beginnings of a shower which would soon settle into heavy rain. Jane shuddered, making a mental note to purchase some oilskins at the first opportunity. She would need them if the weather continued like this. Quickly she reached for the only serviceable mackintosh she had with her and hurried downstairs. Hilda would be wondering where she had got to. The afternoon was well advanced.

She found Mary pottering in the kitchen. She had hoped to avoid her, but she had already poured two cups of tea. 'You didn't have your coffee after lunch,' she said, glancing quickly at Jane, 'What with Mr Karl coming in and the telephone ringing I forgot all about it. You'd better have this now when I've made it.'

Feeling decidedly ungrateful, Jane took a cup from Mary's outstretched hand, adding more milk to cool it down. 'I'd better dash,' she explained, shaking her head as Mary told her to sit down for a minute and take her time. 'I'm late already!'

'Well, that was Mr Karl's fault, I think,' Mary replied calmly as she sat down herself and stirred sugar slowly into her own tea. 'He always brings chocolates back whenever he goes to London, even if it's only for a day or two.'

Against her will Jane found herself remarking, 'It's rather unusual, isn't it, for a man?'

'Probably . . .' Mary frowned contemplatively, glancing up at Jane's doubtful face. 'His father, you see, was never much of a man for presents, not even at Christmas. I think Karl missed out a lot when he was a child.'

Jane's eyes fell to the dark depth of her cup, eager in spite of herself to know why this should be? 'What about his mother?' she asked tentatively.

'His mother?' Mary sounded surprised, and she frowned again. 'His mother died when he was born, my dear. I thought I'd told you?'

'No,' Jane retorted sharply, 'you didn't!' Then, attempting to hide a sudden surge of compassion, she tacked on hastily, 'But of course he had you.'

'Yes, I suppose so.' Mary spoke doubtfully. 'I did my best, but, no matter how good, I don't think a nanny could replace a mother completely.'

'I'm sure you would make up for a lot.' Smiling warmly, Jane slung her coat around her shoulders, and with another reassuring glance at Mary's anxious face made her escape. Her own sympathy for Karl evaporated quickly as she went through the door. She thought fleetingly of his ruthless self-sufficiency. He would never have felt the need of a mother, that one! It wasn't until she reached the dairy that she realized that on the kitchen table there had been no sign of the little jade horse. Mary had never mentioned it, so only one thing could have happened. Karl Grierson must have picked it up and taken it with him.

In the dairy Hilda was cross and flustered and inclined to talk too much. 'It's always the same,' she grumbled, as she sorted bottles. 'Students think they can come and go as they please, and Bill Clark is no exception. Talk about making a farmer! He's too fond of gallivantin', if you ask me! And too la-di-dah by far. Just like you . . .'

Startled, Jane turned her head. Usually she knew Hilda never expected anyone to take her grumbling seriously, but now, for some inexplicable reason, Jane felt suddenly wary. 'What on earth are you talking about, Hilda?' she queried nervously.

'Oh,' Hilda shrugged indifferently. 'It's just your voice—the way you talk. You know fine what I mean. I don't suppose there's anything wrong with it, but it's a bit out of place in a cow-byre. I expect that's why people take notice.'

'What do you mean?'

'Stop repeating yourself, girl, for a start,' Hilda said

110

crossly. Then, with a somewhat repentant grin, she glanced briefly over her shoulder at Jane. 'Do you remember seeing a traveller coming in with Mark Fenwick this morning just as you were going out?' As Jane nodded vaguely she rushed on, 'Well, you might not have noticed him very much, but he must have had a good look at you, and he was certain he'd seen you somewhere before. He comes from Bradford.'

Jane's green eyes widened and momentarily a flicker of fear showed clearly. 'I do remember seeing him,' she admitted slowly. 'But I definitely don't know him, whatever he might say.'

'Oh, he didn't say he knew you, just that he can remember seeing you, and can't place you!' Hilda brushed back a strand of greying hair with soapy fingers. 'Poor man, he was in a state! Annoyed with himself, that is. Asked Mr Fenwick where you came from.'

'And he told him?' Jane's throat went strangely dry as Hilda nodded. Bradford was a big place, but she had helped her mother with a lot of charity work one way and another. Once she had even opened a bazaar when her mother had been ill. It wasn't so impossible that she had been seen. She could only pray that this traveller's memory continued to fail him.

As she had hoped Hilda said flatly, 'He still couldn't place you, but when he comes back he's going to ask you himself, so that's something to look forward to. He's a fertilizer rep, and very presentable!'

Which was cold comfort whichever way one looked at it! Turning rather blindly to put a milk bottle in a crate a few feet away, Jane didn't notice the slippery patch on the floor. Nor did she hear Hilda's warning shout until her feet shot out from beneath her and she found herself holding a broken bottle in one badly cut hand.

'Jane!' Hilda was by her side instantly, her face

111

just a shade less whiter than Jane's. 'Goodness,' she exclaimed, her voice shaking with fright. 'that hand! Are you all right? Can you get up? We'd better get that bleeding stopped right away!'

Through the series of rapid questions Jane struggled numbly to her feet. Hilda, fussing like a mother hen, put an arm carefully around her and helped her on to a stool before reaching for the first-aid box. Jane felt quite sick. Her hair, having escaped the ribbon at her nape, flopped irritatingly across her face and she seemed unable to do anything about it. Her hat, she noticed, had fallen off and lay on the floor which appeared to be heaving up towards her. As another wave of faintness caught her, unwittingly she grabbed at the nearby table with her injured hand, which only made the blood run faster.

'For goodness' sake, girl, be careful!' Hilda's terse exclamation as she put down the first-aid box had a salutary effect. Taking a deep breath, Jane straightened and watched shakily while Hilda poured hot water into a clean dish followed by a liberal splash of antiseptic. Then, with surprising efficiency, she plugged the wound with a large piece of soft dressing and tied a bandage neatly. Wearing an anxious frown she wrung out a small cloth and lightly sponged Jane's hot face.

'There,' she said gently, pushing back the heavy hair. 'Just sit still a minute and you'll soon feel better. I've a flask here. If you wait I'll get you a drink. There's nothing like hot sweet tea.' Quickly she unscrewed the top of her flask and filled it half full, stirring in a pile of sugar before thrusting it into Jane's one good hand.

Gratefully Jane took the flask top and tried to hold it, but her numbed fingers shook and somehow the scalding liquid spilt over her lips. With a small cry of despair she dropped the cup. 'I do seem to be making a mess of things,' she whispered, attempting to laugh but secretly dismayed as she surveyed the broken pieces of glass and spilt tea.

'Never you mind.' Hilda was all patience and concern. 'I'll soon brush that up and I think I know where I can find another cup. Just sit still until I come back.'

Nervously Jane watched her go. This was all so ridiculous! Such a fuss about a cut hand. Hilda must secretly think she was behaving very stupidly. Besides, there was still heaps to do before they were finished, and Hilda also had tea to prepare for her children coming home from school. She must try to get up, then perhaps the room would stop swinging around.

Trying to concentrate, Jane was quite unprepared for the man who came striding in through the open door. 'Hilda!' he rapped out curtly, then drew up sharply, his eyes swerving narrowly to Jane's white face as she sat helplessly on her flimsy perch. 'What the hell have you been up to now?' he ground out.

From what seemed a distance Jane heard the ominous note in his voice and saw the gleam of real fury in his eyes—partly a hangover from their earlier disagreement after lunch, she supposed. A tremor of righteous indignation shot through her. 'I slipped,' she choked, then added childishly, 'I couldn't help it!'

He stood beside her, staring down at her perspiring face as he retorted angrily, 'Why don't you look where you're going? We're short-handed as it is. We can't afford accidents here!'

Hilda, returning with a cup, overheard what he said and tried to intervene, as she told Mary later. 'She really couldn't help it, Mr Grierson. It was that bad patch on the floor.'

But Jane was already struggling to her feet. How she hated this man with his arrogant bad temper! He obviously considered her spineless—and a nuisance. She took a hasty step forward, her green eyes alight with resentment, but before she could retaliate effectively a

113

wave of faintness caught her and, alarmed, she felt herself falling. The next moment Karl had her. In her rumpled shirt and pants she was as slender as a boy and as helpless as a girl, and he swung her into his arms with quite an audible exclamation. As he bent forward to take the weight of her body she felt her lips almost touching his hard brown cheek, and in spite of her dizziness she shivered convulsively. When, apprehensively, she tried to jerk away his hold merely tightened. Dazed, she heard him shouting something to Hilda before he turned to stride out of the dairy.

'Stop struggling!' His voice came taut, matching the grimness of his face, while his arms, steel-like in their strength, held her to him. Through the soft silk of her shirt she could feel the heavy beat of his heart against her own and it was impossible to fight.

Jane took a deep breath of night air, feeling the wind tangling her loose hair, blowing it back from her hot temples. So good, the cool sweet scents from the moors, wild and free, whispering in her ears. But for the pain in her hand and the quivering throb of her pulse she might almost have enjoyed it.

Heedlessly he strode along, covering the distance easily. Unaccountably his head dropped until his chin touched her silky hair and his arms tightened noticeably, as if aware of its delicate perfume. Involuntarily her whole body responded even as she tried to stiffen away from him.

'Be still!' he ordered harshly, as with his elbow he thrust open the farmhouse door.

Twenty minutes later she was sitting in Karl's car, on her way to the village and the doctor's surgery. Disregarding her protests, Karl had insisted that she must have an injection against tetanus and her hand properly bandaged. Mary had insisted too, so there had been nothing else for Jane to do but give in. She went meekly, her hand stinging so sharply that she would gladly have agreed to anything that might relieve the pain. Obediently she had swallowed a generous measure of brandy and done as she was told.

The doctor, a large, kindly man, eyed her intently. 'You seem to have given yourself quite a cut,' he said quietly as he unwound Hilda's bandages.

Karl stood beside them watching but obviously indifferent. All part of the day's work, Jane thought bitterly, as she drew a jagged little breath and stared stoically in front of her. Of course he would be used to people taking chunks out of themselves—there were regular warnings about accidents on farms—but as the last piece of dressing came off she heard his swiftly muttered oath, and, looking down, she saw that the cut ran deeper than she had thought, across the fleshy part of her slender palm.

'You're going to need a stitch or two here, young lady, and a few days off.' The doctor glanced obliquely at Karl. 'Your stable girl has quite a nasty hand, old man.'

She heard Karl reply sharply, 'It's not quite the scratch Jane made it out to be, Andrew.' His voice was low. Perhaps only she caught the undertone of his anger?

Taut, head back, she sat perfectly still as the doctor worked. She didn't need to look at Karl to see the cold hardness of his expression. Recalling his furious exclamation as he had carried her from the dairy, she realized that he had little patience with this sort of thing. An accident which might have been avoided, but for a girl's carelessness. And accidents, as he had asserted, meant inconvenience all round.

'Well, that's it, Miss Browne.' With a slight start she heard the doctor speak as he applied the final plaster. 'You should feel better in the morning, but, as I said before, you'd probably be wiser to go home for a day or two, just in case you feel tempted to use that hand.

Where do you live?'

'Too far away for that, I'm afraid.' It was Karl who answered briefly, as Jane stared at the doctor with startled eyes.

Colour flamed beneath her clear skin as she ignored what Karl said and remarked coolly, 'I don't think that will be necessary, doctor. I'm not really ill, and can always try to do something with one hand.'

'Good job you fell on your left one, then.' Andrew Muir's bushy eyebrows rose as he surveyed Jane sceptically. 'Just remember to go easy, that's all.'

In spite of his advice it seemed to Jane that during the next few days she had never worked harder, although she was forced to admit that the completion of even the smallest task seemed to take twice as long as usual. But she refused to rest. The prospect of sitting around all day contemplating the vulnerable state of her emotions was not inviting. Nervously her mind rejected such a course. She would rather muddle along with one hand than do that!

Karl had said very little as he had taken her home from the surgery that evening. Not that she had really noticed. She had been almost asleep by the time they got back to High Linton, half drugged by reaction and the very effective pain-killer which the doctor had given her. She had felt too tired to protest when Mary had insisted on her going to bed, and followed with a hot-water bottle to make sure she was comfortable.

Mary had only been gone a few minutes when Karl knocked on her bedroom door. One loud, imperious rap, more like a royal proclamation than anything else, Jane decided indignantly as, without waiting for an answer, he strode into her room. Her eyes heavy and clouded with sleep had opened wide to see him standing beside her bed, and she had drawn back uncertainly against the pillows, her long, slim fingers clutching the top of the coverlet. Her heart had pounded so loudly in her ears that she felt sure he must hear.

He had stood looking down on her with weary impatience, lines of tiredness about his mouth. 'Don't worry,' he had said, 'I'm not going to eat you, so don't get alarmed. Nor am I going to lecture you about your hand. I just wanted to leave you something. I found it in my pocket and came back and told Mary that I'd bring it up myself. At the same time I can satisfy myself that you're not much the worse, and all settled for the night.'

As Jane had stared dazedly up at him she heard him place something on her bedside table. 'If nothing else it might serve to remind you of a rather momentous day,' he had finished drily, his eyes scanning her pale cheeks.

Curiously she hadn't been able to look away, not even to see what he had left, although she thought she could guess. Her eyes had remained fixed on his face even while his extreme aridness of his expression, the rather brooding cynicism as he briefly explored her heavy, gleaming hair and the fragile bones of her shoulders and throat, bare beneath the slender straps of her very feminine nightgown.

'At least you don't go to bed with trousers on.' He flicked her cheek lightly, a taunting grin breaking the grimness of his mouth, and reminding her subtly that he had not yet seen her without them.

'I can assure you,' she had managed, with the faintest shadow of a smile, 'that my legs are not bad at all.' Immediately the words were out, to her utter humiliation she had flushed scarlet—like some overgrown schoolgirl, she thought desperately. And somehow, unable to bear any more of his barbed taunts, she had turned and buried her hot face in her pillow, regardless of his low exclamation of mock despair.

'Stop worrying, Jane, or you'll drive me round the bend, and I don't want any more complications at the moment.' His hand clamped down, hard and curiously insistent on her bare shoulder, almost breaking her precarious self-control. Her pulse had began to race unevenly, as it seemed now to make a habit of doing whenever Karl came near.

Then, as if physical contact with her bare shoulder stung, his hand abruptly left her, and he had said, his voice edged sharply, his dark eyes glinting, 'You look enticing enough for any man, but right now I'm keeping my mind on your hand. Just get some sleep, there's a good girl, and I'll see you in the morning.'

Jane heard the door close softly on his last words, a definite decisive click. If he calls me a good girl again, I'll scream, she remembered thinking irrationally, through the choking feeling in her throat. He had gone, as the closed door coldly proclaimed, and she had wanted him to stay. Wanted him with a longing that could barely be suppressed, and he chose to treat her most of the time like a tiresome infant! Sick despair smote her as her good hand went helplessly to her mouth.

Numbly she had turned to see what he had left and was not really surprised to see the little horse. After all, that was the only thing he had to give her. He had still been wearing the same jacket which he had worn after lunch, and must have had it in his pocket. The mystery remained as to why he had ever given it to her in the first place. Was it because, subconsciously, her apparently rootless state appealed to his usually dormant compassion? Well, she didn't want presents from him on that basis. Nor on any basis at all, she decided emphatically, resolving to get rid of this particular present as soon as possible.

Frowning, her eyes shadowed, she continued her silent contemplation until voices in the yard beneath her window interrupted her tangled thoughts. Someone was engaged in an argument. Who, she couldn't quite make out, but down there someone sounded angry. Surely it couldn't be Mary in some sort of trouble? Mark and the two boys were probably out, and she might need help. Anxiously Jane forced her reluctant body out of bed and hastily switched off her bedside light before going quietly to the window. Softly, taking care to make no noise, she moved aside the heavy winter curtains and looked out.

Below her, on the concrete, she saw Mark standing stiffly beside Karl's car, and Karl in the driving seat talking to him through the open window. Mark, with his face half turned towards her, in the moonlight, looked defiant. She couldn't see Karl's expression, almost hidden as it was in the shadow of the car, but, as involuntarily she leant nearer, she caught something of what he said.

'—and I shouldn't entertain any hopes of marrying Lydia if I were you!'

Stunned, Jane eased back into the room, letting the edge of the curtain fall, not waiting to hear more, dizzy again with a different kind of shock from that which she had previously experienced. Karl's words, absurdly, hurt more than the deep cut across her hand, and sent her stumbling almost blindly back over the carpet to her bed.

To Mark, Karl seemed to have said quite clearly, hands off Lydia! His tone of voice had quite plainly stated proprietorial rights, and in some way his suspicions must have been aroused by Mark's behaviour. Or perhaps by some hint or rumour of what had been going on while he was away? Undoubtedly he had been telling Mark in no uncertain manner exactly where he stood!

Poor Mark! Poor Jane! Surrendering to a flood of self-pity, she slid back between the sheets, unhappily aware of multiple shocks which coursed through her body. Never before had she felt the full weight of rejection, and, rather than acknowledge it completely, she sought refuge in anger. How dared Karl come to her bedroom, like a Greek bearing gifts! Lifting her tear-wet face from the pillow, she turned furiously to fling the jade horse across the room, but as her hand reached out and held it she hesitated. Something about the small horse struck an answering chord in her own breast. It looked almost as forlorn as she felt herself. With a half suppressed sob, unable to explain her own actions, she lifted it to her, holding it closely, deriving from it some small measure of comfort as slowly she fell asleep.

It was several days before Lydia came to see her, and when she did come it was not to inquire after her hand. She came while Jane was busy in the kitchen while Mary was out shopping. Jane had discovered that she could do a lot with just one hand, although her injured one was healing quickly and, she found, a good antidote for the persistent ache in her heart which she tried hard to ignore.

'You seem to have a remarkable ability for attracting attention,' Lydia remarked cryptically, after only the briefest of greetings. 'And,' she added coldly, before Jane could speak, 'sympathy!'

Stung, Jane flung her a far from friendly glance. 'Darling Lydia,' she retorted sharply, and with emphasis, 'so, I think, have you!'

As she had expected, her observation had the desired effect. The maid of all work addressing the secretary thus! That Lydia was more than a little affronted was obvious by the slight flush on her usually pale cheeks.

'I don't know what you're talking about,' Lydia snapped shortly, 'If you must talk in riddles you could at least try explaining yourself.'

Jane frowned as she ignored her for a minute while she rather noisily stacked a pile of dishes. Uppermost

120

in her mind was the way in which Lydia seemed to be enjoying the attention of two men. Not that there was probably much wrong with that, but Jane felt that she wasn't being completely honest with either of them, and the knowledge, for obscure reasons, annoyed her. Remembering what she had overheard from her bedroom window, she bit her lip, a puzzled frown on her brow. Could Lydia herself possibly have hinted to Karl that Mark was pursuing her in order to make trouble between the two men?

Not that there seemed much sense in that! It seemed much more likely that she was using Mark in order to incite Karl into more decisive action. Perhaps she was keener than he to be married, even while she enjoyed Mark's devotion.

Jane shrugged impatiently as she turned from the dishes. 'You must excuse my bad temper,' she smiled with deceptive sweetness. 'I thought you'd come to ask about my health, and disappointment always makes me me cross. Then I tend to say the wrong thing, but it wasn't of any consequence. And I'm really in an awful hurry. Mary will be home at any minute, and I've still a lot to do.'

'I really came with a message from Mr Grierson.' Lydia's rather short-sighted blue eyes still glowed suspiciously, in spite of Jane's explanation, and she chose to disregard her pointed reference about her hand. 'I believe,' she went on, 'you're going with him to a horse sale tomorrow, and he asked me to call and tell you to be ready about eleven. We're going off on business today, and he doesn't know what time we'll be back.'

'Oh, I see . . .' Outwardly indifferent, Jane stared at Lydia blankly. There was nothing at all unusual in a man being out with his secretary, but she found it hurt even to think of it. With a kind of helpless anger at her own reactions, she tried desperately to pull herself

121

together.

The blast of a car horn reached them from the road outside, then again, impatiently.

'That will be Karl now,' Lydia cried eagerly, as she blinked uncertainly at Jane's stony face. 'He said he would pick me up, so I mustn't keep him waiting. Although I don't think he would mind waiting for me!'

The snug note was carried in the slight lift of one much beringed hand, and she was gone before Jane could add anything more, if indeed there had been anything more to add.

Over lunch Jane mentioned her day out to Mary. 'Mr Grierson is selling his brown hunter, and I'm to go with him as he might need help. I don't know how long I'll be gone.'

'I shouldn't worry if I were you,' Mary smiled cheerfully as she passed Jane her plate of soup. 'It will be a change. You and Mr Karl both like horses, so you should both have a good day.'

Mark looked up sourly. 'I did suggest to Karl that I went along instead of you, because of your hand, Jane, but he didn't seem to care for the idea. I don't know why as it would have saved you a journey.'

'You know it's not very easy for both you and Mr Karl to be away together,' Mary put in reproachfully, her expression a sharp reminder to Mark of his negligence while Karl was in London.

Noting the guilty flush on Mark's face, Jane said impulsively, 'As manager, Mark, I thought you'd have been able to please yourself?'

Mark pushed his soup to one side, as if it didn't please him any more. He considered Jane's objective remark with a dry grimace. 'In theory, yes, but not in practice.' He laughed shortly as Mary frowned. 'And it's no use shaking your head at me, Mary. You know as well as I do that I'm not much more than a glorified messenger boy!'

122

'You could be more than that, and you know it.'

Jane lowered her eyes so that she might pretend not to see Mary's face, pink with suppressed indignation. She wished fervently that she hadn't said anything. But perhaps Mary was right. Mark didn't really pull his weight. However, at the same time Mary must have some inkling that both he and Karl were attracted to the same girl, and a man didn't work as well as he might with something like that on his mind. Mary, she felt, wasn't being entirely fair.

'We'd best say no more.' The familiar reproof fell from Mary's lips as the two students came in, and with a warning frown she rose to see to their meal. Mark lapsed into a sullen silence, ignoring the friendly overtures of the two boys, showing no particular interest in their conversation, and answering with extreme abruptness their few questions about the job they were busy with.

Sometimes, Jane decided with a resigned shrug, people could be their own worst enemies!

Next morning, Karl's high-powered car, with the horsebox behind it, sped along the grey country road towards Hexham. From the car Jane caught glimpses of high moorlands, bleak fells and grey tarns full of grey motionless water. Beneath overcast skies the sun shone intermittently through low cloud, lighting remote valleys, leaving others in shadow, dark tunnels in hills which faded into the hazy distance. Early morning frost still lingered in grassy hollows, glistening on the last leaves which clung tenaciously to the bare skeletons of trees, a sparkling cold reminder of winter yet to come.

The Military Road followed the line of the Roman Wall with the silvery Tyne in the valley on their right. Housesteads, Chesters, Chollerford. Names which meant little to Jane, but which Karl Grierson pointed out automatically.

'I've heard of Chesters and Housesteads, but the rest I'd forgotten,' she confessed. 'Tourists are very keen on this sort of thing, I suppose?'

Karl laughed, his hands relaxed on the steering wheel. 'Don't sound so disparaging, young lady. We can learn a lot from the past. Besides, for many people it provides an interest, which is a good thing in itself.'

'There doesn't seem a lot to see,' Jane shivered suddenly. 'Just a lot of empty space . . .' She glanced quickly at Karl's dark profile. She felt a need to talk, but not about anything personal. He was too intuitive. He picked up a word here and there with lightning dexterity, forming them into conclusions which one would rather avoid.

She saw his mouth quirk as his eyes turned momentarily from the road, flicking over her wary face with gentle reproach. 'My dear Jane, men are continually writing volumes about it, and occasionally I read some lengthy tome myself, if only to keep up with the latest data.'

'I suppose,' she murmured, demurely, 'that being local it's the least you can do?'

'For your information, Miss Browne,' he replied with a mocking twinkle, 'we are now passing Procolitia in the Notitia—the Roman fort at Carrawburgh. It's really quite extensive, and was first garrisoned by the First Cohort of Aquitanians, and then by that of the Cugernians, and finally in the third and fourth centuries, by the First Cohort of Batavians. Apparently it was found that the gap of eight miles between Chesters and Housesteads left a weak spot in the defences, so this fort was built. I'll take you to Carrawburgh. one day and do my best to explain the intricacies of the Roman defence system.'

'You're laughing at me!' Jane retorted crossly. 'I don't believe such an excursion would appeal to you one bit. I suppose, though, that quite a few people around here must still have some small measure of Roman blood in their veins. Don't you think?' Taunting a little, she glanced at him through the dark density of her lashes.

'Quite possibly,' he drawled, his eyes aiight with amusement. 'They were here a very long time, and we were rather a wild lot on the Borders in those days. Maybe we aren't yet wholly civilised.'

'You'd only need a club,' she returned provocatively.

His laughter rang out, but his voice contained a slightly harder note. 'I might not need even that, if I set my mind to it.' His glance ranged over her with cool derision.

Jane squirmed, oddly unhappy. She was under no illusion. He talked in riddles, but she knew he alluded to Lydia and the thought hurt.

'By the way,' he went on, before she could think of a subtle retort, 'what did Andrew Smailes say about your hand?' His roving gaze lightly touched her neat bandages before returning to the road.

The doctor had seen her hand the evening before, and was pleased with it. 'He said that it was almost as good as new.'

'Good for Andrew.' Karl slanted her a quick look, his dark eyes enigmatical, suddenly watchful. 'Perhaps you ought to have gone and stayed with your brother as he suggested? I'm afraid I didn't stop to think.'

'It seemed you didn't want me to go?' Curiously perverse the question escaped Jane's dry lips.

'Now that you come to mention it, I don't think I did.' His downward glance slid over her again, laconically. 'I might have been afraid you wouldn't come back. And I wouldn't have known where to find you.'

'I must be quite an asset, then, in spite of my injury,' she quipped, applying the only feasible construction to his confusing remark.

'While I'm forced to agree in part, that wasn't quite what I had in mind, Janey. I don't always concentrate on the material aspects, or didn't you know?'

'How could I?' Why did he call her Janey—like that? She was silent as her mind pondered, and his voice tightened angrily. 'Occasionally I'd give a lot to have access to those thoughts of yours, young lady.'

'At least they're not so obvious as yours are sometimes,' she replied sharply, then stopped short.

But the explosion she anticipated didn't materialize. He only laughed softly, although his dark eyes mocked her feeble retaliation. 'Tut, tut, Miss Browne, I didn't realize you aren't completely invulnerable.'

Jane shivered even as a flush deepened over her cheeks. He hinted at something. Surely not her swift indignation at his cavalier treatment a few nights ago? In view of his involvement with Lydia it didn't seem likely, but her heart jolted with a growing conviction. Unhappily she turned her eyes from his face, gazing sombrely out through the window, noting without really seeing the small village through which they were passing. Such an incident must never be repeated, and yet how quickly would such self-denial turn into a delicate kind of torture. She had a sudden, frightening premonition that her time was running out.

CHAPTER VII

Time, especially at a horse sale, goes very quickly, and this one, held in the famous Tynedale Mart, proved no exception. Jane found that, after the horse they were parting with had been groomed, there wasn't a great deal more to do and she was able to concentrate on the actual selling of the horses. Trade was brisk, and many potential buyers, holding off until the last minute in the hope of getting a bargain, were disappointed. Men and women along with children packed the ringside, an assorted crowd and clearly a good-natured one, intent on enjoying their day. Karl, she quickly realized, was well known, and she soon lost sight of him as he was sought out by friends, would-be buyers who obviously valued his opinion.

He sold his own horse for a good three-figure sum and didn't buy another to replace him as she had thought he might.

'I didn't really need Rustler,' he told her when she asked him about it. 'I actually took him in the first place to oblige a chap I knew, and never felt completely happy about him. However, he's completely sound and has gone to a good home.' He nodded lightly to the new owner whom they happened to pass as they were leaving the sale. 'He has a boy about your weight, and I've noticed that he carried you nicely, so he should do well.'

'I think he will, too,' Jane smiled. She liked the look of the boy, a slim teenager who had clearly fallen in love with the horse. 'I must admit,' she forced a light laugh, 'that I was rather shocked at the prices. A horse today would appear to be an expensive luxury.'

'Not by comparison with other things, but definitely not to be purchased by the dozen.' Karl glanced at her with inscrutable eyes. It was after five, and he had an appointment, he said, to see his solicitor in the town. It hadn't been possible to see him earlier. 'I'll see you some time after six,' he went on. 'And we'll have a spot of dinner before we go home.' Without waiting for any comment he named a hotel, giving her brief directions. 'Perhaps you can amuse yourself for an hour?'

With a cool nod he was gone, striding up the street, soon lost in the shadows, and Jane stood gazing after him feeling strangely chilled. This town, the estate, his horses. She was really no part of it. Just a proverbial ship, passing in the night. Suddenly, overwhelmingly, she knew an urgent need to speak to someone of her own. Her mother, perhaps, who might help to dispel this frightening sense of despair. She would find a cup of tea somewhere. There must be plenty of cafés in a town of this size. Afterwards she would ring home.

Plans, she decided unhappily, were easier to make than to carry out. Horses appeared to be terribly expensive, costing a lot more than they had done three years ago. She ought to have kept in touch with the rising prices, but she just hadn't realized. To start a riding school from scratch would cost a small fortune —much more than she had previously envisaged. Even with the help of her grandmother's money it would mean borrowing, something which she would rather not contemplate. And otherwise, what with the stables and the high cost of land, such a scheme would scarcely be possible. There seemed absolutely no point in staying here any longer. She must tell them at Bradford that she was coming home.

In the end she didn't bother with tea. Too dramatically she decided it would choke her. In the telephone kiosk she gave the operator her home number and asked for a reverse charge call, which was easier than having constantly to replenish the coin box, and avoided the risk of being cut off. Her mother usually ran on so!

Rain pattered lightly against the glass windows as she waited for her call to go through, and the concrete floor beneath her feet felt damp and cold. Jane shivered, feeling suspended in space, both mentally and physically, a sort of nomad, isolated and afraid. Normality returned with a sigh of relief as she heard her mother's voice over the line. It might have been her father. It was too early. He would not be back from the factory, but there had been just a chance.

Mums said, before Jane had time to utter more than her name, ' When are you coming home, *chérie* ? '

Straight to the point, her light, quick voice was tinged with impatience. Her impulsive daughter, so like herself at the same age, was a constant source of worry.

Now was the time, Jane knew, to alleviate her mother's fears, and say tomorrow. But somehow nothing came as easily as she had planned. She found herself unable to confess that she must leave High Linton. The words trembled unspoken on her lips, and she could only stare, bewildered, at the receiver.

' Jane dear, are you there? ' Her mother's voice, agitated now, distinctly anxious, reached her from a distance.

' Oh, of course . . . ' Jane murmured faintly, speaking with difficulty. ' How are you? '

' I'm very well, dear, at the moment. But not about me, please! When are you coming home? '

' Mums! ' Jane tried to laugh lightly, dissembling a little. ' You managed without me when I was at school. '

' That wasn't the same, my darling.' The line crackled. ' I'm not a possessive parent and you know it. It's the circumstances which are so—shall we say—unusual. *Ma chère*, to disappear, yes, literally, without a trace. Too, too ridiculous! And your poor father, in a perpetual state of anxiety and crossness, and poor Felix . . . '

Mums was off again! From habit Jane held the receiver slightly away from her ringing ear until her mother calmed down. There was a lot more about Felix.

'Felix,' Jane said coolly, into the first breathless pause, 'doesn't count. I've told you so before.'

'But you count with him, dear. And what sort of a man would he be to give up so easily?'

'I don't love him, Mums. It's quite impossible, you know that!'

'Oh, but I don't, my Jane. Why is it so impossible, I ask you? Felix is a very personable young man, and very amenable. Besides, love isn't everything. There is the business, *chérie*. In France we have a more practical way of doing things, and when everyone is satisfied, then love often comes later. He is so nice . . .'

But I want something more than a nice young man, Jane felt like screaming. I want someone dark and strong, arrogant and bad-tempered. Someone with a name like . . . No, she would go no further. It was foolish to think of anyone in particular. Even so, she couldn't leave High Linton immediately, but that had nothing, just nothing, she told herself stoically, to do with Karl Grierson.

There was Mary. Hastily she clutched at straws. 'The housekeeper where I work, Mums. She's been very good to me. I must give her time to find a replacement. Say about a month.'

'A month!' A small, horrified scream accompanied Mrs Browne's exclamation. Then a pregnant silence, followed by a change of tactics. 'Your papa said that if you rang I was to tell you that he is willing to discuss a riding school. He is prepared, he has told me, to be generous. Surely, then, this is what you want? The good housekeeper must find another woman to help. Do not tell me, *chérie*, that you wash her dishes!'

Tactfully Jane ignored this, concentrating on her father's offer, doubtfully surprised. 'He's probably just dangling a red herring, Mums. Anyway, to tell you the truth, I'm beginning to realize the cost of starting a riding school, and, quite frankly, I don't know if I'll go on with it.'

'Then come home, dear!'

'No, Mums, not yet . . .' Stubbornly perverse, Jane repeated, 'In a few weeks.'

'Well then,' Mrs Browne hesitated, clearly bereft of further argument, 'then I can tell your father that you are coming back to the office—very soon?'

'No, not the office, Mums!' The increasing noise of traffic did not entirely account for the higher note in Jane's voice. 'I'm not going back there! I haven't made any other plans, but it certainly won't be the office.' Quickly she glanced over her shoulder at the small queue of people outside. The excuse, although she felt almost ashamed to use it, seemed too good to miss. 'I must go now, darling. People are waiting to use the phone. I've been here a long time. I'll keep in touch . . .'

As she had never been to this particular market town before, it took Jane some time to find the hotel where Karl had arranged to meet her for dinner. The twisting streets confused her, while narrow corners, their cobbles gleaming beneath the street lights, offered tempting, but usually unrewarding, diversions.

In the end she found it—a large square, unpretentious-looking building squatting in a cul-de-sac just off the main street. Crouched against the November night it didn't look very prepossessing, but although the exterior promised little, inside it was elegantly, even luxuriously furnished.

Karl waited in the foyer. He didn't ask where she had been, but stopped pacing and took her arm impatiently. To her dismay she saw that it was well after six. Her nervous glance flew inquiringly to his face.

'Don't worry,' he answered her unspoken query, drily, as he guided her through to one of the lounges. 'We still have plenty time for dinner.' He pushed her down into one deeply comfortable armchair and pressed a bell for service. Unhurriedly he lowered his heavy body into the matching chair beside her and, when the waiter came, ordered drinks, waiting silently until they arrived.

' Now,' he said sharply, ' drink this.' He handed her a small whisky and soda. ' It will warm you up.' As he reached for his own, his eyes lingered sharply on her pale face.

Jane shivered, hoping irrationally that he wouldn't see. She didn't like whisky, but, as he said, it would probably warm her up. Obediently she took a small sip. Outside the night was cold and she hadn't been near a fire since they had left the estate that morning. On top of this she had found that the telephone conversation with her mother, far from proving satisfactory, had left her feeling more confused than ever, and her fingers tightened around her drink with a sense of total frustration.

He studied her, apparently objectively, as he lay back, his arms stretched at either side of him. He flickered a glance over her face and she felt it come burningly alive. His voice slewed around her. ' You don't have to be always so defensive. I'm not a complete barbarian, you know. There is nothing quite so rewarding as a beautiful woman, but they usualy spell trouble. I've learnt to approach with caution.'

Delivered with such intimacy, the caressing inflection almost shocked her. Anger leapt like a flame, keeping her at a cool distance. Fearfully she moistened her bottom lip. ' I don't think I needed a drink after all, Mr Grierson! ' The decisive snap as her glass hit the table top added emphasis to her brittle words.

His dark eyes glinted, a mocking light in them. ' You're a strange mixture, Janey—impetuous, yet wary, like a young gazelle. Frankly I prefer a touch of sophistication, but we've all got to start somewhere.'

132

Why was he so deliberately taunting? Distractedly she brushed a heavy strand of her hair back from her forehead with fingers which trembled slightly. He seemed to delight in provoking her. The expression in his eyes was disturbing, and his voice had a cutting edge, indicating the hardness of his personality. She seemed to remember a moment when he had also been indescribably tender. Or was she confusing facts with dreams? Staring at his darkly arrogant face she was scornfully convinced this was so.

Anger surged again as she jumped quickly to her feet, tearing her gaze away from him. Then, mindful that he considered her impetuous, she said coldly, 'If you don't mind, I should like to wash my hands before dinner. That is, if you still wish to give me any!'

Retaining what dignity she could, she fled from the lounge, unhappily aware that she left behind only an impression of somewhat juvenile retaliation.

Jane found the cloakroom on the first floor, and after rinsing her face and hands applied a little make-up from the compact which she always carried. Her hair she combed until it shone, untying the ribbon at her nape, letting it fall free, a scented cloud across her shoulders, full of gleaming copper-coloured lights. This seemed to relieve to a certain extent the tension in her head, and she decided to leave it, stuffing the ribbon into her shoulder-bag.

Carefully, because she had the place to herself, she studied her reflection in the mirror, liking her brown coulet skirt. It was in a soft, supple suede with a jerkin to match, and beneath it she wore a silky, toning blouse with a fashionably low neckline. The outfit suited her, bestowing a certain confidence which combated a half-formed wish to flee from the man who waited, no doubt impatiently, in the lounge below. She lingered a while longer, fastidiously tidying, then she flicked off the light and went out into the passage, walking quickly back down the stairs.

He was still sitting where she had left him, and again as she approached his eyes roved over her missing nothing. 'I like your hair,' he smiled lazily as he rose to his feet. 'Why don't you wear it like that all the time—I like it.'

The observation was casual, even mocking, and yet there sped through her person the feeling, beyond analysis, that he was, in spite of his previous remarks, very much aware of her as a woman. Tiny shock waves flooded her mind as her body reacted traitorously. She said nervelessly, without thought, 'It would only get in my way while I'm working.' She moved her head and her hair fell heavy and shining, half hiding her face.

He put out a hand and touched it lightly, his eyes brilliant and mocking. 'Come on, copper-nob,' he said softly, 'you're only pretending to be annoyed. But, come to think of it, perhaps we'd better eat, before I completely spoil your appetite. Our meal is waiting. I thought you were never going to return.'

The dining-room, adjacent to the lounge, was full of oak beams and shaded lights, and the head waiter showed them to a table in a secluded alcove. Jane felt the admiring stare of his eyes over her person as she sat down and smoothed out her skirt.

All through dinner she was acutely aware of Karl sitting opposite her. A small silence hung between them, not to be dispersed by pointless remarks, but her eyes kept slipping away from his hard carved face only to return again, as if unable to resist him. She blinked with a little half audible sigh as he completed ordering from a surprisingly varied menu. Carefully she looked away, seeking something to take her attention, but finding nothing in the softly lit room with its few scattered diners to provide the distraction she sought.

The meal, when it arrived, was delicious—man-sized

steaks, thick and unadorned, with an assortment of beautifully cooked vegetables. With it they drank a fine, smooth Gevrey Chambertin which Karl pronounced perfect. He wouldn't, she thought, have been content with anything less. Jane ate slowly, yet did nothing to disguise the fact that she was hungry. She enjoyed the wine, grateful that it appeared to remove her former despondency.

There was an odd light in the depth of Karl's eyes as he lifted his wine glass, noting the change in her, sensing her lighter mood. 'That's better, Jane. Something happened to you, I think, after you left the sale? If I jerked you back to sanity too roughly you must excuse me. It was for your own good, only don't do it too often. All those small airs of depression seem to arouse the devil in me.'

Her eyes widened as she stared at him, wholly unprepared for the arrogant charm of his smile. 'I think you enjoy teasing me,' she murmured faintly, her lashes suddenly heavy on her pale cheeks.

He gave a brief laugh, curiously deprecatory. 'Sometimes you talk nonsense. But enough.' He leant slightly towards her across the table. 'I may be going away again for a few days. I have an elderly relation in the Dordogne whom I go to see occasionally. I'm afraid I've neglected him lately.'

Impulsively, Jane looked up from her meal, speaking without thinking. 'My grandparents . . .' Then she stopped short, confused, her jade glance flickering away from his narrowed eyes.

He pounced quickly, not permitting evasion. 'You were saying?' he prompted smoothly, his brows rising fractionally in the darkness of his face.

'It was nothing.' Colour tinted her cheeks, proclaiming her duplicity as she half turned away.

But with uncanny perception he grasped the truth, gauging the odd note in her voice. 'Your grandparents are French?' Again his glance flickered over her and he nodded, his intuition too strong.

Jane's colour deepened defensively. 'It's not a crime!'

'Good lord, no. Why should you imagine I should think it was? One of my own ancestors was German— some generations ago.' He frowned at her flicker of surprise. 'Perhaps all traces of my Teutonic ancestry have long since disappeared, but with you it's different. There's something about you. I haven't been able to place it, but I should have known.'

'How could you?' she asked, bewildered.

He leant nearer, his eyes intent on her hair. 'I've seen women in France with hair exactly the same colour as yours. And able to ride as you do. I haven't seen it anywhere else!'

'A coincidence, perhaps.'

'Not that particular shade.' His eyes slipped over her downbent head. One dark eyebrow flared. 'There is also your riding. I've known kids almost born in the saddle who don't ride nearly as well as you do. You're quite something to watch.'

'Oh, please,' she spoke a little breathlessly, glancing up at him. The change in the timbre of his voice struck her and disconcerted she shook back her hair. It would be foolish to deny the sensuous effect this man had on her, but at all costs she must hang on to her equilibrium. 'I've only visited the Dordogne once. My grandparents died before I was born, I'm afraid.'

'Your mother's parents.'

It wasn't a question, although she nodded. He would know of course that the name Browne was scarcely French.

Before she could reply verbally, he tacked on, 'And you never went back?'

This time there was a question. 'No,' she agreed, 'I never went back.' Contemplatively she frowned. 'I must confess I did intend to, but there were other places to

136

visit and somehow I kept putting it off.'

He amended rather curtly, 'You're a much travelled young lady?'

Confused, she shook her head. 'I'm sorry if I've given that impression.'

'Well, no matter.' He spoke with crisp decisiveness. 'Now, it seems, you have an urge to work with horses, which must form a integral part of your make-up, even though you might deny it. Have you ever thought seriously about a riding school?'

Startled, Jane grasped the delicate stem of her glass, feeling it quiver in her nervous fingers. 'Yes and no . . .' she faltered, glancing away from him, secretly hoping that such a vague reply might cause him to lose interest.

'Jane!' Her vagueness apparently irritated, but did not deter him. 'Probably your ambitions have been frustrated by lack of cash. There's nothing so unusual in that! When you talked so enthusiastically about a riding school it started me thinking. I've had such a project at the back of my mind for years, only it's time, not money, that I've been short of.'

Her eyes gravitated to his face, staying there as he paused reflectively, his hand going out to refill her glass despite her small gesture of protest. Interest quickened to active excitement which she instinctively attempted to hide.

'Plenty of people,' he went on, 'need expert tuition and advice and never get it. Pony clubs play an important part, but don't always meet the initial requirement. A lot of children, for instance, could use a riding school, if only to find out if they really like riding, not just the idea of it. It could often spare their unfortunate parents a big outlay in terms of real cash.'

'You couldn't possibly want to bother!' A heavy strand of hair fell across her brow as she leant forward and she brushed it back impatiently, trying to keep her voice on an even note.

'Don't talk nonsense,' he chopped her off tersely. 'Why do you think I bother with Bill and Ben? It's not always easy for pre-college students to find some-one willing to take them on. All I ask is their integrity, and in return, I don't mind putting myself out a bit. Regarding a riding school—at High Linton we have horses not really earning their keep, and plenty of spare boxes in the stable yard. With very little outlay we could provide a service, if only in a small way to be-gin with.'

Rather clumsily Jane's hands fell to her sides. She clenched her fingers tightly to stop herself enthusing with him, to stop herself from suggesting that she would be more than willing to help. Just one word stopped her from impulsively committing herself. Integrity! Hadn't it prompted her decision to leave High Linton in the near future? Better this than face the whiplash of Karl's anger if he discovered the real truth about her circumstances Besides, although he seemed to hint cas-ually that they might run a riding school together, he was probably thinking of the day when he and Lydia might be married and have children of their own?

The thought hurt painfully. She could not forget what she had overheard when he and Mark had quarrelled beneath her window. From any angle to stay here would mean subjecting herself to emotional strain be-yond endurance. Without stopping to examine such conclusions she said quickly, 'I'm sure you're right.' She glanced at him, her face expressionless with a forced indifference. Picking up her bag, she deliberately sus-tained a delicate yawn. 'You must excuse me,' she smiled fleetingly, 'it's been rather a long day.'

The air was suddenly static. Her eyes flew open. In the space of seconds he was remote, a stranger. 'Poor little Jane,' he drawled. 'So full of ideas, but afraid of any personal involvement—a sure sign of immaturity.'

138

Her eyes, the pupils glowing green like emeralds, met his cool, level gaze. She knew instinctively from the sculptured hardness of his jaw that, in spite of the smile, he was in a dangerous mood. His eyes flickered over her, taking in the slenderness of her body, lingering in such a way as to start a pulse beating erratically at the base of her throat. Desperately she sought some negative reply, but could find none that might adequately disperse his barely concealed cynicism.

'I take it,' he observed drily, his eyes returning to her face as she remained silent, 'from that oblique little statement that you aren't interested any more?'

He was giving her a chance to reconsider—and she must refuse. Bleakly she managed a small, resigned sigh, glad that the heavy swing of her hair partly hid her flushed cheeks. 'I'm afraid I change my mind about many things.' Her attempted smile was a dismal failure.

'A woman's prerogative.' His answering smile was hard and brief, scarcely touching his lips.

Jane flinched, panic-stricken for a moment as something smouldered in the depth of his grey eyes. Something unfathomable which told her clearly that he wasn't totally satisfied with her story, and would leave no stone unturned to find the reason for her sudden deviation.

Inwardly dismayed, she pushed back her chair. 'Perhaps you want me to go Mr Grierson?'

'The only place you're going is to the lounge for coffee.' His eyes sparkled with sarcasm as he rose to his feet. 'Don't imagine that my world has come to an end because of one small disagreement. And don't try to run away, that's a good girl.'

Again the hint of a threat in his low voice smote her, clouding the expansiveness of his last remark with dark ambiguity. Quickly she turned from the table to find his fingers on her wrist, drawing her along with him.

'In this hotel it's usually the custom to serve coffee in the lounges. They appear to think that their guests are disposed to linger.'

His tone, and the grip of his fingers, pronounced cryptically that he was not.

It seemed to Jane that although his first surprise at her lack of co-operation had subsided a little, some of the anger still remained.

In the lounge she sank uneasily into her original chair, unaware that the shaded light above her gleamed directly down on her head, illuminating the soft, pure lines of her face. Karl fixed his eyes intently on the delicate tilt of her chin as she drank her coffee.

'When I'm in France,' he said tersely, 'Mark will exercise Hammond as usual. I don't want you riding him whatever the circumstances. You understand?'

'Of course.' Her heart jolted guiltily as she remembered how she and Mark had disobeyed him before.

'Of course!' he mocked, his eyes glinting on her pink face. 'Is it strange that I don't damn well trust you completely, my so plausible Jane?'

She knew a sudden feeling of suffocation as her fingers grasped the fragile handle of her cup. His face was hard and expressionless. There was nothing to indicate that she had even dented the armour of his self-sufficiency. So how could she account for the almost irresistible desire to draw up a list of her sins and confess them one by one? To fling herself at his feet, to gather up what crumbs of mercy he chose to throw down.

Shocked by her own vulnerability, Jane bit her lip until it hurt, her eyes darkening with dismay. Never had she expected to feel this way about a man, least of all Karl Grierson. But following shock came irritation beyond measure. If she didn't pull herself together she would only earn his ridicule. Her precarious self-control would do nothing else but amuse him and, at

140

that moment, she felt unable to stand any more of his mockery.

The silence lengthened, full of a curious tension, but before she had time to defend herself Mark and Lydia walked in through the door.

'Talk of the devil,' Karl murmured ambiguously beneath his breath, while Jane's eyes widened with surprise.

Mark spotted them immediately and came across to where they were sitting, dragging Lydia with him. 'I thought we'd catch you here, old man,' he grinned, his eyes flicking curiously from Karl to Jane, then back again. 'After a horse sale I know you usually stay for dinner. Lydia and I came in for a drink.'

Lydia, fur-wrapped, looking cosy and elegant at the same time, blinked her fair lashes and said, 'We wondered about the sale, Karl darling. Did you get a good price?' Gazing up at him, she smiled sweetly, detaching herself from Mark's proprietorial hand. She ignored Jane, which wasn't so unusual.

'We're just going. And yes, I did get a fair price for Rustler.' Karl stayed on his feet as Lydia relaxed in the chair he held out for her. A small frown creased his dark brows as he stared down at her pink and white beauty.

Noticing the frown, Jane wondered unhappily if he was annoyed to see Lydia with Mark. That he intended leaving right away seemed a clear indication that this was so.

Mark, obviously indifferent in spite of his effusive greetings, lit a cigarette and shrugged lightly through the smoke. 'We wouldn't want you to go on our account, old man.'

'Not at all,' Karl spoke with mock emphasis, apparently deciding to ignore his manager's airy self-confidence, although to Jane's ears his voice held deceptively smooth undercurrents, a subtle warning that

141

Mark might do well to heed.

Mark flushed slightly, evidently not completely insensible to atmosphere even if he wasn't altogether receptive. He hesitated, appearing almost relieved when Karl said smoothly, 'Run and fetch your coat, Jane, while I get these two a drink. I'll join you in the foyer in a couple of minutes.'

Later, going home, Karl scarcely said a word, obviously preoccupied with thoughts which didn't include the girl by his side. Inadvertently his silence hurt, building up an inner tension, sending swift needles of pain across Jane's brow. He was probably thinking about Lydia. She had no means of knowing, but it could be an accurate guess. Everything about this man was growing too personal. For a moment she felt desperately frightened. He stirred alien emotions, flooding her with a curious longing for experiences which she could put no name to.

' I must have a headache,' she uttered aloud, seeking an excuse for such irrational thoughts.

' We'll soon be home.' His conventional reply startled her, not entirely because of the dryness of his tones, but because she hadn't been aware that she had spoken aloud.

Cold comfort in any case! She grimaced wryly, shrinking back into her seat, retreating into silence as the big car ate up the miles. He drove swiftly, without further reference to her aching head. Blindly, at first, she watched the sharp yellow gleam of headlights cutting through the darkness, momentarily illuminating the bare winter branches of trees where they hung precariously over the road. Then slowly the gentle hum of tyres on the hard surface of the road, and the warmth of the interior, had a therapeutic effect, and long before they reached High Linton she was asleep.

Not properly awake, she didn't realize that Karl had drawn up, just past the farmhouse, until he was open-

142

ing her door, giving her a little shake before lifting her
bodily out on to the road.

He stood holding her, his hands on her arms until
she recovered her balance, watching her carefully, his
voice low. 'It's been a long day. You dozed off.'

Still half asleep, she gazed up at him, her eyes wide
as the moonlight caught them, still heavy with tiredness.

'Cat's eyes!' He slanted her a faintly ironic smile.

She considered what he said, slowly, her mind slug-
gish, her sense seemingly drugged, as if unwilling to
return to hard reality. She was scarcely conscious that
he held her. 'You mean because of the colour?' Her
mouth curved, wide and dreaming, and she brushed a
languid hand across her forehead, hazily aware that
the ache had gone.

Suddenly his expression altered, his eyes narrowing
on her pale, smooth face. 'Sleeping Beauty might be
nearer the mark, I think, and you know what happened to her?' Slowly his hand moved up to grasp a
handful of her silken hair, his dark gaze unfathomable
on her moonlit face. 'If I remember correctly someone
had to waken her with a kiss.'

She blinked, her head dropping dejectedly against
his shoulder like a tired child. She closed her eyes, re-
laxing against him, letting the odd tenderness in his
voice wash over her, strangely willing to accept a dream
world.

Gently his fingers left her hair, curving her chin
steadily, tilting it delicately towards him before his lips
descended, warm and softly insistent, on to her own.
Jane's breath caught wantonly in her throat while her
body, totally relaxed from sleep, seemed to melt against
his. Under the pressure of his mouth her lips parted
eagerly, incapable of offering any resistance. She was
only aware of the feverish clamour of her senses, obliterating any desire to escape. A waiting stillness encom-

143

passed her as she responded to the compelling ardour of his hands.

Then suddenly, with an abruptness that stunned even as it jerked her back to reality, he released her. One moment she was in his arms, and the next she was standing away from him, swaying slightly as his voice came sardonically to her ears. 'We seem to be making a habit of this sort of thing, but I'm afraid I'd make a rotten Prince Charming. Anyway, it's time little girls were in bed.'

Unpredictably she began to laugh, a little helplessly, the fire in her veins dispersing into a slight hysteria. For an instance the full weight of his hands descended on her shoulders, clasping them none too gently. Terrified of giving him something else to mock her about, she held herself rigid in his hold. His lips had drained her of all fight, but it slipped through her dazed mind that a girl must hang on to her pride somehow. She must depart with more dignity than she had shown that other evening when he had set out to enjoy himself.

'Of course,' she murmured, as she wrenched herself from his detaining hands, looking anywhere but at that cynical mouth. Determinedly she smiled coolly. 'Perhaps it's I who might be wrongly cast as Sleeping Beauty!'

'Goodnight—and pleasant dreams.' As she turned his taunting farewell floated after her and she heard the car door slam. And like that other evening, not so long ago, her eyes filled with sparkling, traitorous tears.

A bleak wintry shower beat against Jane's bedroom window next morning as she tumbled from her bed. It was still early, but she had scarcely slept and was glad to get up. Fervently she wished she could obliterate the image of Karl Grierson from her mind. His kisses had been deliberate, not premeditated perhaps, but certainly he had seemed to act with intent, determined to arouse

144

her response. The hardness about him was, more than likely, a trace left over from his German ancestors. Well, she wanted no part of it! She certainly wouldn't stay to provide further entertainment! Some time, within the next few days, she would pack up her things and go.

CHAPTER VIII

Jane had read somewhere about the best laid plans of mice and men. A cold, damp wind blew over the countryside during the next few days, tearing the last leaves from the already half-naked trees, and assaulting the roof tops with gale-force ferocity. Following the wind came rain, then periods of black fog from the southeast. Obliterating the hills, it brought visibility down to nil, and chilled everyone to the bone.

On the day that Karl left for France, Mary went down with influenza. It wasn't really surprising as she hadn't felt well since the weekend and a lot of people locally were ill, but it seemed to Jane a sort of anticlimax. So much for her plans to escape! She had hoped to be gone long before Karl came back, but remembering Mary's kindness when she had hurt her hand, she knew she couldn't possibly go now. Not right away, at any rate.

'You'd better go to bed and stay there,' she told Mary firmly. 'I'll ring Doctor Smailes. He'll no doubt give you something horrible to take, but he'll have you up in no time.'

'Mary does too much,' the doctor said dispassionately when he arrived. 'But you try telling her that, young lady, and she's liable to hit you with something. Karl's off again, I hear.'

'France,' Jane replied, although she realized that Mary must have told him Karl's destination. Confused, she stared down at the supply of tablets he was leaving.

'He'll be back.' With matching briefness the doctor nodded, glancing at her keenly. 'Not more than a week or two, I should think.'

It wouldn't bother me if Karl never came back, Jane

assured herself emphatically as she watched the man drive away. Not that she had seen much of him since the night of the horse sale. He had been busy, she knew, with a lot of things to arrange before he went, but she had a feeling that he had deliberately kept out of her way. His emotions, she decided, were involved no more than her own, and it had been sheer folly to imagine otherwise. Stoically she disregarded the frantic beating of her heart when he had gone that morning with scarcely a word.

'You'll have to give me a hand in the stables, I'm afraid,' she told Mark later when he came in for lunch. 'What with Mary being ill and Hilda only able to come for an hour or two, I'll have a lot to do here.'

'You can depend on me,' Mark said quietly—so quietly that Jane stared at him warily. This had always been the trouble. Until now he had been far from dependable, but it might not do to say so.

'That's all right, then,' she nodded, glancing away from Mark's smug smile. A new light of satisfaction shone in his eyes. She couldn't quite fathom it out, but it was certainly a change from his usual sulkiness. She continued, 'Karl won't hear of me riding Hammond. I can handle the horse quite easily, if he did but know it, but I suppose he thinks he's right.'

'He that pays the piper calls the tune,' Mark laughed with a wry shrug. Inadvertently Jane felt a twinge of guilt. She had no right to make her resentment so obvious. Mark was only too ready to appreciate any small criticism of Karl.

'A little criticism never did anybody much harm,' Mark added, clearly reading her thoughts. 'Why so prickly all of a sudden? Karl wouldn't be surprised to know that we mutter behind his back occasionally. Anyway, he does know how I hate his darned horse!'

The slightly aggressive note was there again. Jane slanted him a quick look as she poured his coffee. A

147

phobia was a phobia! He probably couldn't help it.

'I'll have quite a lot to do myself, you know,' Mark grunted as he stirred sugar into his coffee. 'I'll just have to see what time I have. I won't have much while his lordship's away, as I expect you realize.'

Jane sighed as she picked up his empty coffee cup and carried it through to the kitchen. She hadn't missed his slight air of self-importance. Mark was a peculiar mixture. She doubted that he would ever change. However, she told herself with a shrug, she had more urgent things to do than to ponder on the vagaries of human nature.

Busy in the kitchen and keeping an eye on Mary, Jane didn't notice how time was passing until Hilda Dick arrived to do her afternoon stint. Simultaneously the telephone rang and she flew to answer it.

Someone wanted Mark, in a hurry. 'It's important that he gets in touch with us as soon as possible,' the girl, obviously a secretary, announced when Jane replied that Mr Fenwick was out. 'Mr Ridley would like to speak to him. Perhaps you would ask him to ring us back as soon as you can get hold of him?'

Politely Jane promised to do just that as she carefully wrote down the name and number. The name seemed to ring a bell, but she couldn't immediately place it. She must try to find Mark, wherever he might be. It probably wasn't as important as all that—everyone appeared to be in a fearful hurry these days—but she might as well see where he was.

Hilda had no idea, although he had called to have a word with her husband after lunch. 'Try the steading,' she suggested. 'No doubt you'll find him somewere, or, if all else fails, I would try the Hall. Miss Lydia's down there.'

Jane glanced at her swiftly with a quick frown, but made no comment. 'As you say,' she agreed, ' he's bound to be in the steading. Afterwards I may take

Guinevere for a canter, so don't expect me back for an hour.'

But Mark was nowhere to be seen. She searched through the steading, working her way around to the stables. He might be out on the estate. As he had pointed out, there was plenty to do. She wished now that she had taken more notice of Hilda's hint that she should try the Hall. Apart from Lydia, there were many reasons why he should call at Karl's office. Perhaps it might be a good idea to take Guinevere in that direction. They had to go somewhere and it wouldn't take long.

There was a bridle-path which Karl had shown her some weeks ago. It went through the fields between the farm and the Hall, an easy ride for a horse. Occasionally, she knew, Karl used it himself when he returned home for lunch. There was a small stable behind the courtyard which was convenient.

Today, Jane felt there was no necessity to ride into the immediate grounds. Instead she tethered the little mare to a post and walked through the shrubbery, then through a small wicket gate to the rear of the office. It was only as she was closing the gate that she glanced casually towards the office window, and drew back, startled. Mark was there all right, and so was Lydia. Lydia, held fast in Mark's arms.

Jane wasn't so much surprised by what she saw as shocked. Hadn't Lydia hinted all along that Karl was in love with her? Jane had thought it just a matter of time before they announced their engagement. Karl's own dalliance with herself on odd occasions she put down simply to a certain sex antagonism which seemed to exist between them. Probably not uncommon between a man and woman, but often nothing to do with a man's more serious intentions. Mark, in a way, she excused to a certain extent. He had confided long ago that he was in love with Lydia, but was uncertain about

149

Lydia's feelings. Well, there seemed nothing uncertain about her feelings now! Her arms were locked tightly around his neck, and she appeared to be returning his kisses with complete abandon.

Numbly Jane moved towards the door, knocking loudly, deriving some small satisfaction as she visualized the startled reactions within. Owing to the rising wind, and their absorption in each other, neither must have heard her approach, and were probably unaware that she had seen them. Quickly, with a perfectly expressionless face, she related the telephone message to Mark, noting sharply that though Lydia was now seated sedately at her desk, a flush of colour flared across her cheekbones. Guilty colour, Jane decided hotly. Yet as she stopped speaking she also noticed their swift exchange of starry glances. Mystified, she turned away.

'Thanks a million, Jane,' Mark called after her, as she walked back through the door again. 'I'll get in touch with Mr Ridley at once, but I know what it's about.'

'Which is more than I do!' Jane muttered, half under her breath, as she went to collect Guinevere.

Returning to the stables, Jane decided that she must confide in Mary. Not completely. She mustn't mention having seen Lydia in Mark's arms, but she most somehow reassure herself that there was nothing going on behind Karl's back. Not that she had any great sympathy for him! Her heart flooded with bitterness. He was surely too much of a philanderer himself not to realize that women were sometimes quite capable of playing the same game. But there was something unaccountable about this whole affair which filled her with unease. For her own peace of mind she must try to find a few answers. At the worst Mary could only say no.

Mary recovered fairly quickly, but it was several days

before she was well enough to sit up in bed and talk. Jane didn't mind the extra work involved in looking after her, although she would readily have admitted that she found the continuous cooking and dusting tedious. When she had stayed off work to nurse her mother there had been a cook in the kitchen and plenty of extra help about the house.

Propped up against snowy pillows, Mary's eyes brightened as Jane arrived with her tea one afternoon. She waved towards the chair by her bedside. 'Come and sit with me, Jane, while I have my tea. I'm afraid you're spoiling me disgracefully.'

Rather reluctantly Jane sat down. Now that the opportunity which she had looked for was here, she felt a curious reluctance to take advantage of it. Uncertainly she stared with fixed attention into the old-fashioned grate.

'There aren't many left nowadays,' Mary told her, following Jane's intent gaze and construing it incorrectly. 'People have them taken out, or boarded up. Mr. Karl wanted to take that one out, but I wouldn't let him. Carrying fuel upstairs is hard work, of course.' Her eyebrows lifted ruefully.

Jane smiled as she considered the cheerful, flickering fire. 'Bill and Ben have brought up all the coal, so I don't think you need worry about that. Actually, I'm going to miss it when you're better. It's been lovely here in the evenings with the curtains drawn.'

'You're much too young to be sitting here with me, dear.' Mary frowned, even while she looked at Jane with some affection.

Jane shook her head, moving tentatively in the firelight, noting the dancing shadows on the walls. She knew a sudden urgency to make a start somewhere, to ask about a few of the things which troubled her, but she wasn't at all sure where to begin.

She concentrated on a leaping shadow. 'I've wondered, Mary, why you didn't stay with Karl at the Hall. Surely it would have been easier?'

Mary took a slow sip of her hot tea, seemingly a little amused by Jane's slightly apologetic tones, but not annoyed, as Jane had feared she might be. 'I left the Hall when I married, dear, and when my husband died of a heart attack I decided to stay here. I thought it wiser to leave things as they were. Besides, someone has to be here to look after the staff.'

'The Hall seem rather—well, sort of threadbare,' Jane offered, still groping.

Mary sighed and stirred uneasily, as if what she saw in her mind's eye bothered her little. 'Mr Karl doesn't bother much, I'm afraid. Money isn't the problem, but a lot of the rooms are under dust sheets. He rarely entertains. Besides, a house always needs a woman's touch.'

'He might get married.' Jane flushed, unhappily nervous. Her casual remark had a trace of urgency about it.

'He might, dear.' Mary didn't seem to notice the betraying colour beneath Jane's skin. 'He certainly hasn't lived like a hermit, if that's what you think.'

Jane's flush deepened at the barely concealed implication. She didn't need Mary's reassurance that Karl was a man of some experience. Yet confusion precipitated her next words. 'I thought perhaps Lydia . . .?'

To her surprise Mary emphatically shook her head. 'I don't know why you should think that, Jane. Lydia will marry Mark, Especially now.'

'Mark?' Jane's averted gaze flew back to Mary's face. In spite of Mary's former reassurance she still felt doubtful. 'But what will Karl say? I mean,' she floundered, 'if he were fond of Lydia himself?'

'You do go on.' A frown creased Mary's brow as she regarded Jane patiently. 'I'm quite sure that Mr Karl isn't particularly fond of Lydia. Certainly there isn't any emotional involvement. As for the other, well, Mark is his cousin, so why should he say anything?'

'His cousin?' Jane's eyes widened with astonishment. Her heart lurched painfully. She had had no idea!

Mary gazed at her white face with some concern. 'Surely you knew?'

'No, of course I didn't.' Jane's clear voice faltered, 'How could I when no one told me?'

Mary was obviously surprised herself. 'It just never occurred to me that you didn't know. I thought Mr Karl would have mentioned it when he interviewed you that first day. Although, I suppose, there was no reason why he should.'

'It does seem to explain a lot of things.' Jane bit her lip uncertainly. 'I've often wondered why Karl puts up with Mark's inefficiency, to begin with?'

'Perhaps I can explain briefly, dear. It's certainly no secret.' Mary carefully placed her finished tray on the table by her side, then turned back to Jane. 'Mark's mother, you see, was widowed early, and left penniless. She was old Mr Grierson's sister, but she wouldn't come back here to live, although she did allow her brother to help her. She died, not long after him, while Mark was at college, and Mr Karl sort of inherited him along with the estate, if you know what I mean.'

'Karl appears to have been left with quite a few people to look after,' Jane noted quietly, as Mary paused.

Mary nodded. 'That's just it, dear,' she said wryly. 'Mark came straight here as manager. After Lydia's father died we hadn't one, and Mr Karl thought it would be a good idea. But I'm afraid Mark has always been very unsettled, refusing to live at the Hall and things like that. He would certainly never tell anyone that he was Karl's cousin if he could help it. Very prickly, and full of false pride, I've always thought.

153

However, we did think that when he and Lydia fell in love that he would settle down. And then what happens? He refused to take their relationship seriously, saying he had nothing concrete to offer. He refused to consider that he had a good future here, although he never attempted to look elsewhere. He's been quite a problem, I can tell you!'

Intrigued, Jane asked breathlessly, 'Why has Karl bothered, then, do you think?'

'Because men like Karl Grierson do bother,' Mary replied, firmly. 'He couldn't see much happiness for Lydia if Mark refused to grow up. Then, when he returned from London that last time, he learnt indirectly that the two of them had been looking over a farm. This particular farm has since been sold for much more than they could afford. But it did give Mr Karl an idea.'

'Idea?' Jane waited expectantly, her eyes intent on Mary's face.

'He's decided to let them have Low Linton. That's the farm across the valley which he incorporated with this one when the tenant retired. He's to let them have it for a moderate rent, and will stock it for them as a wedding present. He was going to wait a while, but something, I don't know what, seemed to precipitate his decision.' Mary smiled, as if it pleased her somehow that everything had been brought to a satisfactory conclusion. Not, Jane was convinced, because she was getting rid of Mark.

Jane said, suddenly remembering, 'There was a man on the telephone after lunch. He wanted to speak to Mark urgently. A Mr Ridley.'

'That would be the solicitor,' Mary nodded. 'Mr Karl told us before he went that an agreement was being drawn up, and that Mr Ridley would be in touch with Mark as soon as it was finalized. I expect Mark was delighted when you told him, although you

154

wouldn't know what it was all about.'

Jane shook her head as a patter of rain against the window brought her slowly back to earth. For some people, she thought bleakly, a happy ending was still possible, but it could never be so for herself—or Karl. Mary obviously didn't believe that Karl was in love with Lydia, but Jane herself was not so sure. She couldn't forget what he had said to Mark beneath her bedroom window!

She became aware that Mary waited eagerly to hear what Mark had said. 'He was thrilled,' she answered quickly. 'I could see that, even if, as you say, I didn't realize what it was all about. I expect I was on the wrong track about Karl and Lydia.'

Mary went on smiling, looking altogether better as she watched Jane jump to her feet and gather up the tea tray. 'I think perhaps Lydia did dream occasionally of being mistress at the Hall. One day, perhaps, if Mr Karl didn't marry. But I also think that Mr Karl might have his own ideas about that!'

That mysterious statement was something to ponder over during the next few days, but it brought little reassurance. Mary might dismiss any hint of an affair between Karl and Lydia with a few casual words. Jane, however, found she couldn't disregard her former impressions so easily. Inwardly unhappy, she found the strain intolerable, and was more determined than before to go at the first possible moment. With this in mind she made the most of her time left with the horses.

Mary was up and about again, almost her old cheerful self. Doctor Smailes was delighted with her. A week in bed, and good nursing had worked wonders. She looked better, he said, than she had looked for some time. Today, after tea, she was going to a meeting of the Women's Institute with a friend. She had asked Jane to go along with her, but Jane made a hurried excuse, a quick decision going through her head. With Mary out of the way she would have the house more or less to herself. Mark, she knew, was picking Lydia up in Newcastle, where she had been shopping, Jane suspected, for her trousseau. Bill and Ben would be going down to the village pub. There was a darts match. She could pack, then pop the suitcases beneath the bed. No one would notice. Jane looked after her own bedroom. Such a chance might not come again, and she must go at the weekend. Before Karl arrived home at the end of the following week. It seemed suddenly imperative that she should be gone. Mark would have to manage the stables himself during the intervening days.

Mark had promised to spare her an hour this afternoon, but if he didn't hurry it would soon be dark. Jane frowned, glancing towards the wintry-looking sun, already creeping sluggishly towards the horizon.

Hammond, catching her impatience, stamped restlessly in his box. Jane called to him to be quiet while she saddled Guinevere. Momentarily, as she finished her task, she laid her head against the little mare's side. The horse turned to look at her with a soft whinney, and swift tears stung the back of Jane's eyes. Determinedly she blinked, refusing to let them fall. Horses, like dogs, could sense one's mood, and pain was insidious, catching one unawares. To know that she might have helped Karl run a riding school was pain beyond bearing. Tremulously she gazed around the stable as if seeing it for the last time.

Mark arrived at last, rubbing his hands together, complaining about the weather, his fair skin reddened by the frosty wind. 'It looks like snow,' he grinned. 'Getting ready for a white Christmas!'

Jane felt herself flinch. She didn't want to think about Christmas. Christmas was a time for love, for closeness and oneness, not for being miles away from

156

the person one loved. As she would be. 'Mark, I wish
you would hurry!' she snapped at him. 'I have the
most awful headache and times getting on.'

'Sorry, old girl.' He glanced at her persuasively, his
good humour remaining intact. 'I've been down at the
Hall. Quite a lot of things to see to.'

'I bet,' Jane retorted, so shortly that Mark stared
at her in alarm, while the colour deepened in his cheeks.
Nothing had yet been said about him and Lydia getting
married. Mary had said that they were waiting until
Karl returned before announcing their engagement. But
Jane could see by the renewed effort which he was putting into his work that he was almost a reformed
character. Besides, now that she came to think of it,
hadn't Lydia been in town all day?

'I'm sorry, Mark. Don't take any notice of me,' she
mumbled, ashamed, at his crestfallen face. 'I guess my
bad mood has nothing to do with you. Here,' trying to
make amends she passed him Guinevere's reins, 'you
go ahead. I'll catch you up.'

As usual she rode Hammond, although she hadn't
intended doing so this afternoon. Mark was genuinely
nervous of the horse and Jane took pity on him, disregarding Karl's last instructions. He would never know,
or when he did she would be gone.

Up on Hammond the world was her oyster. Even now
the feeling of exhilaration never failed. But Mark was
right—it was cold. Why hadn't she worn her jacket?
Her thin sweater did nothing to kep out the icy winds.
'Let's gallop,' she shouted to Mark as she caught him
up. 'I want to get warm!' The wind tore through her
hair, loosening the tight coils, tangling long strands
across her pink cheeks.

Mark agreed, shouting back above the wind. 'We
could go right over the hill, along by the road. It's a
good ride.'

Jane nodded, hiding a smile. She guessed why he

157

wanted to go there. From the road one could see the farm which he was getting, in the bottom of the valley. For Mark it would be like viewing the promised land. Well, good luck to him! Not that she was supposed to know anything about it.

'Come on then, I'll race you!' Her low laughter reached him on the wind as Hammond, responding swiftly to the slightest pressure, broke recklessly into a wild gallop, soon leaving Mark, an indifferent rider on the smaller horse, far behind.

That was how Karl Grierson saw her—a distant figure tearing headlong across the fells as he returned home late in the afternoon from France. Hammond stood out unmistakably against the drab winter colouring of the rough moorland, and the car skidded slightly as he frowned, applying sudden pressure to his brakes.

Unconscious of his presence, Jane was enjoying the exhilaration of the ride, the blood singing through her veins like sparkling wine, temporarily anaesthetising her unhappiness. Guiltily she was aware that she rode too quickly, but this was glorious country, wild, mostly unfenced, and Hammond was as sure-footed as a mountain goat. Behind her, Mark was forced to go more carefully.

Seeing that she was nearing the road, she steadied Hammond carefully, but was scarcely aware of the car or the man beside it until she was nearly on top of them. Then, as her glance curved carelessly sideways, shock sluiced over her in an icy torrent. Karl stood tautly against the fence, just a few yards away, watching her.

Too suddenly she tried to stop, her hands tightening apprehensively on the reins as Hammond reared indignantly. Like Jane, he had been enjoying himself and it was some minutes before she could control him. 'Steady, old man!' she spoke sharply. To her utter chagrin the horse suddenly recognised the man on the

158

road and plunged towards him.

As if anticipating his movements, Karl was over the fence in a flash, grasping the plunging horse firmly, his decisive action bringing Hammond to an abrupt halt. As the horse stood quietly Karl's hold slackened, and his eyes dark with anger turned to Jane's face. His mouth was a tight hard line. 'I distinctly remember telling you not to ride this horse!' His tone indicated a barely controlled fury.

Jane's newly acquired warmth fled as her eyes met those of a man staring up at her. The wind still blew cold, with a flicker of snow in it, but his eyes scorched, blotting out the chill. Tremors ran convulsively, as the shock of seeing him back so soon numbed her mind. Helplessly she uttered the first thing that entered her head. 'Mark doesn't like riding him, and you know it.'

Her trite remark added fuel to the fire. He waited an apology, not an upbraiding, but she had never had to cope with a man as furious as this before. It was outside her experience.

'I'll have somebody's head for this,' he ground out, 'be it yours or that of my dear cousin!'

'We didn't expect you back so soon,' she choked inanely.

'Obviously not!' He treated her remark with the contempt he clearly thought it deserved. 'I seem to have caught you at a disadvantage.'

'Mark had nothing to do with it . . .' Frantically Jane tried to think straight. In his present mood Karl seemed capable of anything. He could even decide that Mark was too irresponsible to have the farm! Then there would be no wedding. Such a catastrophe must be avoided whatever happened. Her own fate didn't really matter, but Mark's whole future could be at stake. 'I persuaded him,' she said, 'to let me have Hammond.'

'Will you be quiet!' His eyes flicked her face, burn-

159

ingly alive, yet cold with indifference. Hammond reared, as if sensing his displeasure, and Karl spoke to him curtly, his whole attention fixed unrelentingly on Jane.

She dared not dismount. Apart from the fact that she seemed rooted to the saddle, she had a curious conviction that if she did slide to the ground he would shake her, like a disobedient child!

As if reading her thoughts, and wishing to justify her worst fears, he snapped tautly, 'Get down off that horse.'

It didn't seem logical to explain that she couldn't move. That the tone of his voice, his whole demeanour, endued a certain paralysis, against which she seemed to have no defence. Did he have to treat her in such a outrageous fashion?

Anger stirred slowly, then flared, motivating her subconscious reactions, as he repeated his command in even terser tones. Mark was coming up behind—she could hear the soft thud of hooves. Whatever happened a quarrel between the two men must be avoided. She must provide some sort of distraction.

Apprehensively disregarding Karl's furious exclamation, she jerked Hammond's bridle from his restraining fingers, digging sharply with her heels. Almost physically she could feel the full force of his anger as she fled. She had seen him many ways—angry, tolerant, laughing, always vital, but never as coldly furious as he was now. The glittering lights in his dark eyes seared her and she turned her head blindly as she went, her hair long and streaming across her shoulders. She was safe for the moment. He couldn't reach her. Like a prisoner escaping she refused to look behind her. Fervently she hoped that Mark would have the sense to say nothing at all.

Back at the stables, she had Hammond unsaddled and in his box before Mark appeared. Looking singularly dejected, but not completely cast down, he trotted carelessly into the yard.

'Karl wants to see you as soon as you finish this evening, darling.' Soberly, with a wry grimace, he passed on the message, glancing at her curiously as he dismounted.

Jane had scarcely had time to regain her breath and felt her cheeks grow distinctly paler. On the way home some of her ill-temper had disappeared, but there still remained at the back of her mind, a niggling resentment. Mark, however, seemed relatively unscathed, which was something. She had half expected that Karl might come after her immediately. This way she might have time to compose herself a little, but it would all amount to the same thing in the end. 'Of course,' she shrugged, acknowledging Karl's order with a nod, while refusing to relieve Mark's curiosity.

'I say, Jane . . .' Hesitantly, and with rather schoolboyish embarrassment, Mark stared at her. 'It was awfully good of you to sort of square me with Karl. His good opinion means a lot just now, but that shouldn't make me any less of a man. I shouldn't have let him swallow the impression you gave him, that you went off on Hammond when my back was turned. I should have had the guts to tell him that I'm an arrant coward so far as Hammond is concerned. I even held back deliberately when I first spotted him on the road. I should have . . .'

Jane smiled, throwing up her hands, warding off a further flow of abasement. Her pink lips curved, in spite of her inner desolation. Mark, in a humble mood, was a stranger. She wasn't sure that she didn't prefer his usual airy confidence. 'It wouldn't have made any difference,' she pointed out soberly, 'whatever you had done. Karl was in an awful temper. The fault was mine as much as yours, and I think I know exactly what he's going to say.'

Later, as she stacked dishes after a late tea, after

161

seeing Mary off to her meeting, Mark reminded her not to forget about seeing Karl.

'You're to go along to the Hall,' he said. 'I haven't seen him since, but he did say he would be there all evening.' Mark's brown eyes were suddenly anxious as she glanced at him coolly. 'You will go, won't you, Jane? I can guess, of course, that it's going to be about this afternoon, and if you would like me to come with you, I could go before I look for Lydia in town.'

Jane, remembering that he had quite a long journey in front of him, shook her head. 'I'm sure it won't be anything I can't cope with, Mark. And I'd rather go alone.'

In any case it wouldn't have been feasible, she decided, as he turned away. Karl and she spoke the same language in spite of superficial differences. His was the more dominant personality, but, unlike Mark, she would refuse to be trodden into the ground completely. Mark was better out of the way. Besides, if she and Karl were about to part in a thunder of dissention, she would prefer no witnesses. Her own heartache would be witness enough.

Mark tried again as he went out. 'I'm giving Bill and Ben a lift to the village. I could drop you off at the Hall as I go?'

Again Jane shook her head, smiling in an effort to reassure him. 'Stop worrying, Mark. There are one or two things I must do first. I'll enjoy the walk and I promise I won't be late. If you don't hurry you're going to be late yourself, then Lydia will wonder where you are.'

Having an impulsive nature was rarely a blessing, Jane thought ruefully, when an hour later she arrived on Karl's doorstep. The wind, which had blown all day, had dropped, to be replaced by heavy rain which had fallen like a cloudburst on her hatless head as she had walked down the drive. To add to her dismay, the light jacket which she had thrown on in a hurry was soaked, and her hair clung wet to her scalp and dripped down her back. Cross at her own stupidity, she groped about the huge oak door, finding the bell. exerting more pressure with her numbed fingers than she would normally have used. She ought to have let Mark bring her. It did nothing for a girl's confidence to realize that she must look like a drowned rat!

It seemed a long time, but actually it was only a few minutes, before anyone answered her imperious ringing. The door opened abruptly and Karl appeared.

He ushered her in, proceeding her across the hall and into the library.

There followed an ominous silence. Scarcely daring to look, Jane glanced slowly at the man beside her. He had discarded the town suit which he had been wearing, and in its place wore a comfortable pair of slacks and a silk shirt. A dark silk scarf was knotted carelessly at his neck, and on his feet he wore a pair of the finest suede shoes. Two wall brackets, set against the chimney-breast behind him, provided the only illumination, shadowing his face in darkness as he stared closely at Jane.

The light from behind his head lit mercilessly every feature. His eyes leapt over her, noting her wet hair, her soaked jacket, her eyes, the pupils widely dilated by rain and darkness. Her slightly defensive, faintly incongruous figure. 'Why didn't you have the sense to bring Mary's car?' he ground out. 'She wasn't using it this evening.'

Cars—umbrellas! Jane swallowed convulsively, her eyes, beneath their thick lashes, a rain-washed green. Karl's mood had obviously not changed. Mary had told her that he had called, but she hadn't said anything about the car. 'I expect she forgot to suggest it.' She shivered, suddenly colder. 'I only saw her for a few seconds.'

He made no attempt to conceal his scepticism. Before Jane could draw another breath, with two strides he was beside her, whipping the wet jacket from her shoulders, the swift movement of his hands brooking no argument. Taking no notice whatever of her flushed indignant face, he grasped the offending garment firmly and disappeared through the door. He was back almost as quickly with a clean white towel which he tossed to her impatiently.

'You'd better dry yourself on this,' he exclaimed. 'And don't forget your hair. It seems to be making a fine mess of my carpet!'

Jane swung around to face him, almost grabbing the towel, blinking away tears of temper. All he worried about was his carpet. How arrogant could you get! Beneath her jacket her soft shirt seemed to have escaped the worst of the deluge, but was damp and clung to her figure. Her satiny jeans were damp, too, but would dry, as she knew from past experiences. Her hair was the worst. Throwing caution to the winds, she removed the remaining pins, then throwing the huge towel around her head, rubbed vigorously. Almost visibly she made an effort to ignore his caustic regard.

With the vigorous rubbing came some measure of control. Through the dense whiteness she could feel his eyes watching her, taking stock, while he prepared, no doubt, his speech of dismissal. The cool cynicism in his eyes proclaimed it. With arms upraised she stopped suddenly and stared at him stiffly, she said, 'There wasn't any need to provide this. I don't imagine your business with me will take long. I could dry out much quicker in the farmhouse kitchen, and there would be no risk of ruining your carpet.'

His eyes glinted, catching and holding her gaze decisively. 'I'm not in any particular hurry, Miss Browne,' he said smoothly. He ignored her remark about the carpet.

Jane tried again. 'I wouldn't want to waste your time.'

He turned away from her, hands deep in pockets, his shirt stretching taut across his broad chest. 'It seems that you do have a conscience after all, Miss Browne. We've already wasted considerable time. I'm not particularly fond of being kept waiting. I was just about to ring the farm to see where you were. Didn't Mark give you my message?'

Her arms aching, Jane lowered the towel, tossing back her still damp hair. It fell straight and heavy on to her shoulders, clinging softly to her nape as she nodded. 'But you forget that my time is not my own,' she retorted coolly, resenting the imperious not in his voice.

'You finish at six.'

She lifted her face and looked at him levelly. 'You forget that I help Mary, which means that I'm not always finished at six. It's often much later.' Which was a slight exaggeration, but it might help his next Girl Friday.

'Fine,' he snapped tersely, clearly unimpressed. 'And that's enough of the Cinderella act for one evening.'

'You don't believe me?' Inconsistently she defied him.

'You talk too much—I've told you so before.' Frowning, he cut her off ruthlessly as he reached to remove the towel from her taut fingers. Before she could resist he took her arm, thrusting her none too gently into a deep chair by the fire. 'Just sit there for a minute and dry out!'

For a moment his grip seemed to tighten as she glanced up at him startled. His breath fanned her cheek, and her mouth quivered uncertainly at the dangerous glint in his eyes. Seeking distraction, her hand went to the tangled strands of her hair, aware that her heart gave a frightened leap, then beat agonisingly fast. In the pause which followed she dared not trust her voice.

'The proverbial Eve . . .' Observing the unconsciously provocative movement of her long white fingers, he drawled, deliberately mocking, 'You've got glorious hair. You don't need to draw my attention to it.'

Her eyes blazed as her body stiffened. A defiant kind of fury flooded her being. She sat quite still, delicately fastidious, anger swept her, a spark of temper which brought her to her feet. 'I won't stay here . . .'

His hand descended, a weight on her shoulder. 'You will. For another ten minutes. Or longer, if I choose.' His voice held the merest hint of a threat, as he forced her down again into her chair, taking no notice of her shimmering, outraged eyes.

CHAPTER IX

A silence dragged itself on. Jane stared into the dancing
flames, feeling Karl's hand, still on her shoulder, the
pressure lighter now, but full of abstruse warning.

'Calm down,' Grimly, Karl spoke to her 'You're
definitely not running away. Stay and face the con-
sequences. Whatever your faults, I don't think lack of
courage is amongst them.' With a dry grin he poured
two brandies, one of which he passed to Jane. 'I
always seem to be dozing you with this, but I don't
want a case of pneumonia on my hands.'

He would be referring to the night she cut her hand.
Rather warily she accepted the drink. It stung her tight
throat, but was curiously warming. She might even
have enjoyed it if she hadn't been aware of the sentence hanging over her. Studiously she stared into the
fragrant liquid, her dark lashes lowered. His face swam
above her, darkly enigmatical, sharpening the pain in
her breast. He looked more vital than ever after his
sojourn in France. Something quite positive and un-
controllable flared through her.

Swiftly she averted her head, not wishing that he
should see her struggling with her thoughts. His eyes
were inscrutable. A low flicker of dislike replaced the
turbulence within her. Sometimes he seemed something
less than human. Despairingly she concentrated on the
room. She hadn't been here before, and like the rest
of the house, although it was comfortable enough, it
lacked a woman's touch. Her heart ached suddenly for
Karl's lonely childhood, even while she found the small
boy of her imagination difficult to connect with the
decisive, self-contained man in front of her.

Uneasily she stirred. This brief respite could not go
on for ever. As soon as she had finished her coffee he

would tackle her about Hammond. Already, from his expression, she could see that it was uppermost on his mind. His patience was limited. As soon as she appeared to have recovered from her soaking, it was clear that he was ready to quote from a long list of her misdeeds. Hammond would be only one of them.

One could sit under a guillotine for just so long. Knowing a moment of panic, she glanced up at him, her mouth and her wide green eyes the only colour about her. Clenching her hands into tight fists, she drew a deep breath, attempting to speak lightly. ' You wanted to see me about Hammond? '

' What were you expecting? ' His voice held a thread of steel, warning her to go carefully.

She looked at him steadily under the wide wings of her brows. ' I'm sorry I left you so abruptly. Perhaps you frightened me.'

He gave her a long look in return, his own eyebrows lifting. ' A devious sort of apology,' he replied sardonically. ' I admit to being furious, but I did allow myself time to calm down. Why was it, do you think, that I didn't follow you to the stables? '

' I'm sorry,' Jane repeated inanely, quite unable to cope with the question. A sense of pride had forced an apology, even though he wasn't satisfied with it. What more could she say. Utter wretchedness welled up inside her, moving her head helplessly, causing her hair to fall heavily across her face as it dried in the heat of the fire. Quickly she pushed it back, starting to struggle to her feet. ' I think it would be better if I went.'

He laughed shortly, a mocking sound, his eyes brilliant on her white face as she stood before him. ' I've almost exhausted my supply of patience,' he said forcibly. ' Don't you possess such a thing as intuition? '

Trembling slightly, she half-turned to put down her empty glass. His attitude was something unexpected, rocking her already unsteady composure. His arrogance

168

and temper were familiar, but not this. His satire was beyond her, clothing her in doubt. 'I don't completely understand what you mean,' she murmured. 'It might have been better if you'd followed me to the stables. We don't all have your calculated self-control!'

He stood very still, his eyes fixed broodingly on her, not visibly moved by her half audible attack. 'My dear Jane, you can't always judge a man by his actions. The chances are that had I followed you there, my actions might have outweighed my better judgment.' His glance roamed, frankly exploring where her crêpe blouse clung softly to her figure and the tiny pulse beat unevenly at the base of her throat. 'You're very young, very untouched. A man has only so much self-control.'

'You talk as though I'm scarcely out of the schoolroom!' Her voice throbbing with indignation, quivered. 'And what you imply is a lot of nonsense. I came here to talk about a horse, or—rather . . .' Her voice faltered as her eyes fell, away from his glittering ones.

'Go on!' he taunted her, his voice hard and abrupt, rather terrifying. 'The more I see of you, the more convinced I am that you've been thoroughly spoilt, somewhere! Not that that explains the attraction which exists between us. But while it might not be explained, it can't be ignored, and you know it.'

A shimmering mist danced between them. Jane tried to focus, but the cold rush of his words burnt the intervening space, beating like fire through her brain. Trembling, she put pale, slender fingers to her temples, pushing hard. His eyes remained fixed on her face and she felt giddy, her mind blank. 'Please, Karl . . .' Her voice was a mere thread of sound.

'Please, Karl!' he mimicked, coming nearer, towering above her, his height and breadth of shoulder never more apparent. He lifted his hand, and she flung her head back instinctively, her heart beating so fast that no other sound came to her ears. But, instead of throw-

169

ing her out as she feared, his hands caught her shoulders, sliding down to grasp the soft flesh of her arms, pulling her towards him with a savage look of controlled violence.

'You couldn't fail to understand this,' he mocked softly, as his arms went around her.

'Don't!' Wildly she heard herself protest, but he took little notice. His eyes were like daggers, slashing over her. Jane's head snapped back on her slender neck as his lips descended. A force which parted hers in a kind of elemental hunger. Ineffectually her hands pushed against his chest as she twisted her head, attempting to escape, but it was impossible. He held her easily, with superior strength, the soft weakness of her body seeming to incite him further. Her temporary struggles were ignored if, indeed, he was even aware of them.

Then, as before when he had kissed her, the blood started to run like fire through her veins. His mouth hurt hers, he had no mercy, and, all the while she could feel his hand, moving slowly, insidiously through her hair, tugging it gently from her forehead and neck, his fingers warm against the bare skin of her nape, pressing her ever closer. Excitement flared as her body responded to his intimate touch. He could be dangerous, she knew that, but suddenly she did not care. Through the thin silk of his shirt she could feel his heart striking into hers, and her own arms clung, her hands going up to his shoulders, to his face, feeling a muscle jerk at the side of his mouth.

Before, his kisses had been something purely physical, but now, with her love for him surging to the surface, there was a deep urgency about her response which had previously been missing. She could feel every muscle in his hard body. She was wreathed in flames, and the violence of emotions she had not known she possessed.

Then slowly the pressure of his mouth eased. He
170

spoke, his voice slightly thick against her lips. She thought he said darling, but couldn't hear properly. Completely disorganized, she tried to speak, her lips quivering as she attempted to escape him. But he didn't allow it. His arms tightened again, bruising her with his hard strength as his fingers came beneath her chin. His fingers were insistent yet curiously unhurried as he forced her head up, almost as if he knew she was completely at his mercy.

Instinctively Jane struggled. 'You're a brute!' she managed to gasp, her hands trying to thrust him away. He only laughed, the sound low and mocking, disbelieving as his lips went unrelenting to her neck. Mercilessly he sought the pulse that beat wildly at the base of her throat, inflamed by the way her body pressed to his as, her resistance forgotten, she returned his kisses with a kind of helpless, primitive desire which matched his own. Fire merged with her senses, bringing total surrender as his lips left her throat and returned to her mouth with bruising pressure. Ecstasy, which entered the realm of pain, overcame her. And with resistless technique he stilled her every ineffectual movement, sending all coherent thought from her mind.

Then suddenly he was holding her away from him, his breath slightly uneven, warm on her cheek. His eyes narrowed grimly on her dazed face, darkly sardonic as her wide, uncomprehending gaze met his. His was the superb discipline which enabled him to say deliberately, his body taut, 'Before we go any further, Janey, I wonder if you mind telling me exactly who you are?'

Ever afterwards Jane remembered that moment. How shock flooded through her as his words struck her like particles of ice, and how her mind groped wildly for an answer, and none came. The transition had been too sudden. She could only stare at him mutely, the large dilated pupils of her eyes, merging into a misty, translucent green. Had his kisses been deliberately intentional? Her lashes fell, fanning out against her cheeks. Then she forced herself to look into his face. Unwisely, driven by some inner desperation, she retorted, ' All this as a means of satisfying your curiosity? Perhaps you intended to make me suffer because of a perverted sense of frustration about Lydia? '

' Now what the devil are you on about? ' She had no warning of his sudden anger, or that she was laying herself open to a whole load of complications which she couldn't hope to contend with.

Mutely she stared at him, but before he could repeat his question the telephone rang, the loud stringent ringing exploding into the fraught atmosphere like a time-bomb. For one palpitating moment she thought Karl was going to ignore it, then slowly, without taking his eyes from her tense face, his hand went out and he took the receiver from its rest. ' High Linton, 315,' she heard him say automatically.

With almost superhuman effort, Jane took advantage of the interruption, wrenching herself from his still firm clasp. The turmoil inside her receded a little as she steadied herself against his desk, yet her eyes returned startled to his face as she heard him bite off a short exclamation. There must be bad news. Nervously her hand went to her bruised lips as she observed his rather grim expression.

After a very few words he thanked the caller and rang off, turning back to Jane as he did so. For one pulsing, pregnant moment he stared at her, his eyes full of a glittering contemplation. Then, decisively, his manner changed, as with a half smothered sigh he thrust his own affairs to one side. He said grimly, ' That was the police. Mark has been involved in an accident with another car. They've taken him to Hexham hospital. I'd better get over there right away.'

Jane's eyes hadn't left his face, and her pulse, which had slowed in the last few minutes, jerked again painfully. She didn't waste time expressing inane sympathy, but asked sharply, 'Was Lydia with him?' At the thought of it her cheeks grew cold. If Mark had been on his way home she must have been!

Curtly, Karl nodded, adding, 'But she isn't hurt. Apparently she was thrown clear. Of course she'll be shaken. They aren't sure about Mark. It's often difficult to judge the extent of the injury until one gets to hospital. He might not be badly hurt, but, as I said, I must get there immediately. You'll come with me, of course.'

It was more of an order than a request. Unhappily Jane stared down at the desk. He looked pale, his voice full of underlying anxiety. Did he still care for Lydia? Overwrought, she thought of the way he had just kissed her, the way he had held her in his arms. But then he had only been trying to find out who she was!

'Come on.' Unaware of her hesitation, he picked up a bunch of keys and impatiently took her arm. Quick panic overtook Jane as she knew what she must do. Swiftly she protested, 'No, Karl, I'll stay here. Mary will come home and wonder where I am.'

He stopped, his fingers taut on her arm, his eyebrows drawn together. It was a weak excuse and didn't sound convincing. 'We could leave a note. I might need some help with Lydia.'

Always Lydia! Deliberately Jane shook off his restraining fingers. While he was away she would pack one case and go. It might be the only chance she would get. Besides, she might not have the strength to go later. When Karl returned she must be gone. Confession might be good for the soul, but so far as he was concerned, any confession she might make would be totally unacceptable. The thought of his contempt stiffened her wavering resolution. She hadn't the courage to face it.

'Please,' she whispered, as he waited, 'I don't think

I'm very good at that sort of thing. Someone else must help you.'

For a short space of time his dark face looked strangely withdrawn, yet he didn't explode as she had half expected. To her utter surprise and despair he put his arms around her again, gently, his terseness gone as he noted the faint air of exhaustion about her, the tremulous quiver of her soft, unguarded lips. His own lips quirked at the corners, but softly, as he bent his head and kissed her—so lightly that afterwards she imagined a feather had touched her mouth, leaving a warm, trailing flame across her cheek.

'Okay?' His arms fell away and his face receded abruptly. Across the room he turned at the door, waiting for her to go through. 'You're probably right. I'll drop you off at the farmhouse.'

Quickly she followed him, forgetting to collect her jacket as she climbed into the car beside him. Silently he drove along the drive, while she sat nervously, her hands clenched tight, not allowing herself to think, trying to grasp those last few moments of unbelievable tenderness, so that she might keep them for ever.

But, as he drew up to let her out, he said enigmatically, 'I'll see you tomorrow, Jane. We have a lot to discuss. I think we can start where we left off, although I promise not to ask too many questions.' His eyes were dark, intent on her face as she gazed back at him, her dark red hair spilling wildly about her shoulders.

'Goodnight, Karl,' she said in a choked little voice, as she fled from him on silent feet into the house.

Jane arrived home late the following afternoon. It had all been too easy, she decided bleakly, as she walked in unannounced, and suffered her mother's rapturous embraces. No one had tried to follow her. Such an idea she knew of course to be ridiculous, as no one could possibly know where she had gone, but at the same time she was aware of a deep feeling of abandonment which, she told herself, was even more illogical.

After leaving Karl, she had packed a case and gone quickly, leaving a note for Mary, expressing her regrets and thanks. Explaining that she was forced to borrow her car, but would leave the keys with the station-master, who she knew would return them with the postman in the morning.

Everything had gone so smoothly. A night in a large impersonal hotel, the simple task of picking up her own car from the garage, her journey down the motorway home. There had been no necessity to cover up any traces. She had felt herself disappear into thin air so completely that she had scarcely believed it herself until she found herself standing on her own doorstep.

She had only stopped once on the way down, for a quick cup of coffee, and to ring the hospital to inquire after Mark. She was told that Mr Fenwick had a broken arm, and was suffering from shock, but that his fiancée, Miss Cleaves, was quite unharmed.

She had put down the receiver after thanking the ward sister, with a feeling of definite relief. She hadn't, the previous evening, stopped to consider how she might have felt if Mark had been seriously hurt. As it was, Karl would no doubt dub her a hard-hearted bitch, if he forgave her so far as to think of her at all!

Now, drinking delicate china tea, Jane tried to concentrate on her mother's many questions. 'It's good to be back, Mums,' she said, not altogether untruthfully, as she sought to satisfy her mother's curiosity. 'The job I've been doing was dull, darling. It wouldn't interest you one bit. Not your line, I'm sure.'

'We must fatten you up, dear,' Mrs Browne noted Jane's figure with an anxious frown. 'And your cheeks —where has all your colour gone—and your hair! I must make an appointment with Raymond in the morning . . .!'

Jane nodded abstractedly, trying to concentrate, rather ashamed to find that she was paying scant attention to what her mother was saying, but unable to rid herself of the feeling that she was a stranger in a strange place. The room they sat in was a charming apartment, with two long windows, and wide stretches of smooth fitted carpet. They were surrounded by fine paintings, and the fragile, expensive bits and pieces which her mother collected so casually. In spite of being rather delicately fastidious herself, Jane felt traitorously that she didn't belong here any more. She knew, with a sudden surge of dismay, a deep longing for Karl's huge, sparsely furnished mansion, and an even deeper longing for the man himself.

Her father, like her mother, was delighted to see her. Dropping his evening paper, he gave her a great, bear-like hug. 'High time you did turn up,' he grunted with typical bluntness, his eyes keen on his daughter's pale face. 'You don't look much better for the change, as far as I can see.'

She had expected interrogations, reprisals, but none came. She was surprised, relieved, then grateful. Apart from the odd remark she might only have been away a few days. Her father talked a good deal, and laughed, conveying in no uncertain terms that he'd missed her, but refrained from asking many questions. Too busy with his own business to attach much importance to hers, Jane decided with rueful affection, not completely convinced that his attitude was prompted out of regard for her feelings. It was simply that he was prepared to forget about her escapade, and was pleased that she seemed more than willing to do the same. He obviously presumed that she was ready to settle down, to marry Felix, and co-operate with his future plans.

Her mother was much more curious, being eager to know exactly where Jane had been, whom she had been with. And anxious to know why she had left in

176

such a hurry. Her insistence Jane found almost as hard to bear as her father's indifference. 'It was just a job, Mums,' she repeated, for what seemed to be the hundredth time. 'Rather ordinary. I'd rather not be reminded.'

If only it was as simple as that, Jane thought rather desperately, as the days changed into weeks, and she came home one evening alone from the office. Her own car was being serviced and she had refused a lift with Felix. She had gone back to the factory, but didn't intend staying there permanently, whatever her father might say. She hadn't really intended going back at all. Her own restlessness had driven her to it. She felt tired —her sleepless nights were responsible for this—but she found it quite impossible to sit at home doing nothing. Her mother didn't need her any more, in spite of her protests. The holiday in Canada had worked wonders; besides there was a daily woman and cook to cope with all the chores.

During her first few days home, Jane had felt she was going slightly mad. All the time she had found herself thinking about High Linton, remembering a curious affinity with the grey skies and fells of the north. At night, in bed, she could still hear the wind moaning through the pine trees, and often felt herself longing for the sight of Mary's homely face. Nor did it help matters that every tall, dark man reminded her of Karl. Then her heart would start and shake until she saw that it wasn't him at all. She loved him, but had thought she would forget. Now she doubted if she ever would, and the knowledge brought increasing despair.

This evening, just a few days before Christmas, she was wet through. It had been foolish to get off the bus at the other side of the estate when it was raining so hard. The twisting drive of widely spaced executive houses didn't provide much shelter. Not that much was ever needed. The residents of Elm Drive all had cars, mostly two or three. In a downpour like this, all they might ever require was a long, bone-handled umbrella to see them safely from their luxurious limousines into the office.

But the rain, beating against the bus window, had attracted Jane irresistibly, bringing back poignantly that last evening at High Linton. For the first time since she had left she allowed herself to go over every detail of that last hour with Karl. Unaware of how wet she was getting, she had loitered, and now she realized rather foolishly that, like that other evening, she was drenched! Her hair was soaked, and water ran down her back.

'Ugh!' she shivered impatiently, quickening her reluctant footsteps. She had forgotten that her parents were going out to dinner. Fortunately she wasn't included in the invitation, but George was picking them up and they would be wondering where she was.

Quickly thrusting her long, wet hair back from her face, she turned into their private drive. Hurrying, she didn't notice the low, sleek car parked in the shadows as she thrust open the front door. For one blinding instant the hall seemed to swing around, as she saw the man who stood there talking to her father and mother. They were dressed, ready to go out, and the man whom they were conversing with so attentively was Karl Grierson!

Jane's heart deapt like a flame in her breast as her fingers groped blindly for the edge of the table behind her. How had Karl discovered where she lived? Her eyes widened as they flew to his. His tall figure loomed above her, his dark eyes directly on her. She gazed up at him transfixed. The shock of it was more than she could stand.

'Mr Grierson has called with the clothes you left behind. And about other things,' Eustace added smoothly.

178

'He's been telling me about his father's cousin in the Dordogne!' Mrs Browne bubbled over excitedly. 'I used to know the district so very well . . .'

Jane nodded blankly, oblivious of her mother's pleasure, tearing her eyes away from Karl's darkly sardonic face. Fear made her tremble helplessly, and her attempted smile was a dismal failure which no one appeared to notice. Using shaking fingers, she began to unbutton her coat, forcing herself to speak to Karl directly. 'Thank you,' she murmured, 'for bringing my things. I expect you're in a hurry to continue your journey. You must be on your way to London. You mustn't let us keep you.'

A few feet away Karl's expression darkened. 'Allow me.' With elaborate politeness he was at her side, exactly as he had been a few weeks ago, removing her rain-soaked coat. As she protested faintly, his eyes went over her, and she flinched at the flicker of anger which smouldered in their depth. Agitation swept over her, and the need for self-protection.

She started to speak, but simultaneously came the loud tooting of a car horn outside. 'That will be George,' Eustace said. 'You must excuse us.'

At the same time she heard her mother explaining as she gathered up her wrap, 'Mr Grierson is to stay tonight, Jane. Cook will serve dinner at seven, so you'd better hurry and change.'

Jane scarcely heard her mother's polite farewell, or her father's assurance to Karl that he would see him later. What on earth had Mums meant when she said Karl was staying? Surprise and dismay eddied through her, but before she could ask, George tooted again, impatiently, and they were gone, leaving her alone with the one man she most dreaded seeing.

Yet, for an instance, while he was close to her, she knew an almost overpowering urge to turn and press her face against his chest, to touch any part of him.

179

And, almost as if he reciprocated her feelings, his jaw clamped tight, and the muscles of his hand went rigid as he held her coat.

Then suddenly he wasn't near her any more. Disposing of her dripping article of clothing, he said suavely, 'Your parents suggested that I stayed, and I find it convenient. I have no intention of going on to London. Now, might I suggest that you follow your mother's advice and go and change. It might seem presumptuous if I offered you a towel in your own home.' His eyes dwelt ironically on her wet head, clearly indicating that he remembered another evening, and similar circumstances.

Jane flushed, even as she shivered. 'You're a sarcastic beast,' she said jerkily, hating to be reminded as his eyes flickered over her with relaxed insolence.

Unimpressed, he leant forward with a briefly mocking laugh, slightly threatening. She caught his expression apprehensively, and unable to trust her own fragile defences, tilted her chin and walked quickly past him to the stairs.

All sorts of questions tormented her as she dressed after a quick hot bath. Almost she had decided to go to bed, a sense of outrage at his satire possessing her. But she suspected that if she did so, he was quite capable of coming up and dragging her out, and such an undignified procedure didn't bear thinking about.

There seemed little doubt that he meant to read her a lecture. Possibly he considered it long overdue—there had been a glint in his eye which, in retrospect, filled Jane with alarm. But, she decided scornfully, only a man of his calibre would take advantage of his victim's hospitality in order to humiliate her.

Bracing herself with angry indignation, she continued with her toilet, deliberately taking her time. Even so, when it came to the moment to go downstairs again, her courage almost failed her. Swiftly she glanced in the mirror. Instantly she regretted wearing one of her prettiest dresses in an attempt to gain some small measure of confidence, but it was too late to change now. Crazily illogical, she wondered what he would think. He had never seen her wearing a dress like this. Anxiously she stared at her reflection. The soft, fine jersey clung seductively to her waist and hips before falling in supple folds to her feet. The neckline was low, and the colour, a soft aquamarine, suited her, accentuating the whiteness of her skin. Yet in spite of the mirror's reassurance, she felt oddly keyed up, experiencing a wild desire to flee.

The dinner gong sounded, and she hesitated no longer, turning from her reflection in the glass to switch off the light with impatient fingers. If she stayed up here any longer she would soon be a nervous wreck. Much better to go down and face the music. She might even be quite irrational and regard this evening as a sort of bonus, gleaning a kind of perverted pleasure from Karl's company. She might never have such a chance again!

He was waiting in the drawing room and his dark head inclined a little as she came in, his cool glance sliding over her burnished head, her understated but beautifully applied make-up, with a hint of satisfaction. Beneath his enigmatic regard her hands shook, and she clasped them in front of her tightly so that he might not see, as they went in to dinner.

Throughout the meal, which was served in the smart, Regency-style dining-room, they spoke very little. Jane felt that she might well have been eating sawdust, and her usual fund of small-talk seemed curiously dried up. How she longed for some of Karl's sangfroid! One topic seemed to dominate her thoughts, pushing everything else from her mind, but she found it impossible to speak of it during dinner. It was only when they returned to the lounge for coffee that the question tripped uncontrollably off her tongue end.

He sat opposite her as she poured coffee. 'I can't help wondering how you found me.' Warily she passed him his cup, glancing up to find his eyes fixed on her pale face. 'Perhaps,' he suggested, his voice slightly edged, 'you're annoyed because I didn't come sooner?'

Jane quivered with rage. How dared he suggest such a thing? He must have a rare conceit of himself! 'That's quite ridiculous!' she denied hotly, her green eyes sparkling. If only she didn't feel so upset, so disturbed inside, she might have thought up something more completely annihilating.

He seemed not one whit put out, his confidence supremely intact as he surveyed her disparagingly, attacking her without mercy, his coffee untouched. 'Now that I've found you it would be foolish to go home without hearing your explanation. I will admit to being curious. Who wouldn't be? Behold in person the penniless little orphan, miraculously transformed into a provincial princess. A modern fairy tale, unless I'm mistaken.'

His eyes like rapiers raked over her. Jane swallowed with difficulty. He looked big and dark and slightly menacing. As she watched him, her heart beat suddenly fast with a new apprehension. With an effort she wrenched her gaze away from his, staring guiltily down at her hands. 'You exaggerate,' she murmured weakly.

'But you did say your father was a working man?' Again his voice was laden with sarcasm. He was surely furious with her!

Jane shivered, even as she flushed defensively. 'So he is,' she cried. 'He works as hard as anyone in the factory.'

He dismissed her protest, his lips curling. 'You wouldn't expect me to agree with you, surely? He's certainly no ordinary working man. He holds a string of companies as long as my arm. We talked before you came in.'

'You can't hold me responsible for that!'

'No. But I can hold you responsible for the entirely false impression you gave.' His voice was coolness itself as he stared directly at her. 'Don't try to wriggle out of that! However, that's only one of several questions I want answered, otherwise I should never have bothered to find you.'

He hadn't changed. He could still be beastly, pursuing everything to the bitter end. 'You haven't told me yet how you found me?' Confused, she sought to satisfy her own curiosity.

She felt his eyes upon her, stripping away her vulnerable defences, making her feel faintly ridiculous, his mouth drawn in a tight line. 'If you must know,' he said hardily, 'it was dead easy. Some of the clothes you left behind had shop labels. Then Mary and Hilda recalled that a rep from Bradford had clearly remembered seeing you somewhere. It was a relatively simple matter to contact him, and, with a little additional sleuthing, you weren't a mystery any more.'

She could not answer him. It was so simple. And she had imagined that she had left no clues! How he must have laughed at her! Slightly hysterical laughter hovered on Jane's lips. Nervously she gulped it back, swift colour flaring beneath her skin. 'I've been home almost three weeks!' Impetuously her voice rose, faintly ludicrous. 'You didn't hurry.'

'You're not reproaching me?' His voice was silky, his eyes speculative on her flushed cheeks.

'No—I mean . . .' Momentarily startled by the truth, she shrank away from him. He was playing with her, she knew it. A cat and mouse game. And she wasn't the cat.

'You might recall,' he cut in drily, before she could go on, 'that Mark had an accident?'

Jane sat tautly still. The censure in his voice stung

and frightened. ' I did ring. The very next morning. I was told that his arm was broken.'

Karl's thick brows rose as his dark, sceptical eyes searched through her. 'You aren't completely without compassion, then?'

'You enjoy making fun of me!' Jane's breath came quickly as she looked away from him around the room.

His glance sharpened. 'There are things I enjoy more. But you must have known that I'd be too busy to leave High Linton until Mark was at least well enough to keep an eye on things. And now,' he said softly, 'you can tell me why you left that night in such an almighty hurry?'

The line of attack was now into her own camp! Jane's pulses raced, and a shimmering mist appeared to dance around her. She would have expected him to know the answer to that one. Unhappily she had no desire to put it into words. Childlike, she had thought that by ignoring such a situation it might go away, but she might have known that she could never escape such an inquisitor. Her lashes fell as she moistened her lips. 'I seem to have caused you a lot of trouble,' she whispered, opening her eyes and looking full at him. 'You must have some idea why I left so suddenly. Deceitfulness is one of your pet hates, and I'd led you to believe that I was as poor as a church mouse. I just didn't realize my mistake until it was too late.'

'Too late for what?' Their eyes met and clung, as his voice, full of hard vitality, smote her. Then, when she didn't reply, he rose, reaching her with one stride, his hands coming down on her shoulders jerking her up towards him. He caught her brutally against him, his mouth a fierce hard line, crushing her to him, taking no notice as frantically she tried to turn away. Her head went back with a soft moan against his shoulder.

'Stop playing with me, Karl,' she cried desperately. 'Must you have your pound of flesh?'

'If I must,' he laughed softly into the loosened coil of her hair, burying his face in the clouded scent of it, while his fingers traced the line of her throat, coming smoothly to tip up her chin, so that she was unable to hide the tremulous shaking of her mouth. He drew an audible breath, staring down at her mouth and the heavy, betraying sweep of her dark lashes, and then he was kissing her—not with the tentative, experimental kisses of their previous encounters, but with consummate passion, and there was no question at all of her resisting him. Ecstasy flooded her body, lifting her into a world she hadn't known existed. There was no pretence any more. She allowed him to do as he willed, as a strange weakness possessed her limbs and desire unfurled in her wildly.

Then, as if aware of the danger, he drew away, his caressing hand stilled, his eyes intent on her drugged face. 'Suppose,' he said gently, 'we start at the beginning?' Swiftly he pulled her down with him on to the settee, his arms still around her. 'It's always the most satisfactory way, I've found.'

Jane stirred. She could feel the possessive control of his body and her head flopped against his shoulder, as helplessly she tried to do as she was told. 'Karl,' she began brokenly, 'I saw your advertisement, but when I arrived at High Linton Hilda Dick as much as said that you wouldn't consider anyone with wealthy parents. This should explain almost everything. You apparently considered such girls just wasted your time. But I wanted to work with horses, to have my own riding school, and my father refused to help me. This meant that there was only my grandmother's legacy, so it seemed doubly important that I had some experience. It was even conceivable that I might not like the life . . .'

'And you saw my advert and never stopped to think.' He twitched her small pink ear-lobe sharply as she

185

averted her head.

'I know,' she trembled, trying not to lose her self-possession. 'But I was feeling fed-up. Nothing seemed to be working out, and I was on holiday with nowhere special to go. Then I saw it in the paper. It seemed a rather heaven-sent opportunity, and not too far-fetched to work.'

Breathlessly she tried to pull away from him, but he would not let her go. 'Not before you tell me honestly why you left,' he insisted gently.

The gentleness in his voice was Jane's undoing. With a half suppressed sob, she buried her hot face against his chest. She could fight him no longer, and impetuously she whispered, 'Because I loved you. When you kissed me I knew. I also knew you would never forgive me . . .'

'So you ran away!' His arms tightened as he looked down at her, but there was something like anger in the depths of his eyes. 'You could have tried telling me about it. Your impulsiveness operates in the wrong directions.'

Tersely she rubbed a tear before it could run down her cheek. His arrogance was quite something! 'Maybe it does,' she spluttered, 'but you don't love me, and I'm not completely emancipated. There seemed no point in baring my soul. But I think,' she finished, in a blazing rage, 'that I hate you now, so it doesn't matter.'

'Oh, no, you don't.' She hated the way his teeth gleamed as he threw back his dark head. 'And you'd better not, my darling, as I told your father just over an hour ago that we're to be married. Only I had to confess to him that I hadn't asked you yet.'

Jane gasped as she listened. He must be teasing! 'You couldn't possibly want to marry me?' she said painfully. 'Judging by the way you've acted this evening.'

'You mean because I didn't haul you into my arms the moment you came in?' The devil in him read her thoughts and laughed at her through his dark eyes. 'You must make allowances for human nature, Jane. I wasn't prepared to forgo some small degree of revenge for the agony I've been through since you left.'

'But,' her eyes flew, puzzled, tear-bright, to his face, 'you told my father . . .?'

Suddenly he relented, his eyes sobering as he bowed his head. 'I told your father that I loved you, Janey, if that's what you're waiting to hear?' His mouth was on hers again and all coherent thought ceased. The full weight of his body crushed her as his hands slid around her back, moulding her body in its thin soft dress to his, making her overwhelmingly conscious of his need for her. She had never been as close as this to him before, and the room around her seemed to be slipping away as her hands went up behind his neck and she returned the smouldering pressure of his lips.

Then, with a heavy sigh, he was putting her away from him, but only slightly, and she put a dazed hand to his face, wanting the moment to go on for ever. 'I imagined you were in love with Lydia?' she murmured, as the thought intruded from nowhere.

He sighed as if inwardly praying for patience. 'Wherever did you get that idea?' he asked drily, his eyes still absorbed in contemplation of her tremulous face.

'I overheard you telling Mark beneath my bedroom window that he shouldn't entertain any hopes of marrying her.' Jane flushed unhappily. 'I didn't intend to eavesdrop, but I couldn't help hearing. You sounded so cross.'

He grinned after a moment, as he recalled the incident, but obviously not alarmed by it. 'If you'd been a little quicker in reaching your window, darling, you might have heard exactly what I did say. I told him

187

that not until he mended his ways should he entertain any hopes of marrying her! Now do you understand? '

' Oh.' Jane felt extremely foolish—but how could she have known? She fought to keep calm, remarking bleakly, ' But you didn't love me then.'

Karl groaned, bending his head to touch the corner of her mouth. ' Perhaps not quite as I do now, but I was well on the way towards it. I hired you, darling, very much against my better judgment. You see, in spite of your brazen attempt to deceive me, I sensed a mystery, but even then I couldn't resist you. Then, when you turned up, apparently on very good terms with Mark, I had a definite feeling that I had made one big mistake. Hence the fury. Hadn't I been trying to get Mark and Lydia straightened out for ages, then, just when it seemed that things were working out, it appeared that I might have upset all my well-laid plans myself. Mark,' he added, rather grimly, ' has always been too easily diverted by a pretty face.'

Her laughing eyes scanned his face. ' That's all I was? '

' Don't be silly, girl,' he shook her lightly. ' Why do you think I doubled my efforts to find Mark a farm? He's always been in love with Lydia, and this accident seems to have sobered him up completely. Marriage, a farm, and a wife whom he loves. I think he suddenly realized what he almost lost. I don't think we need worry about those two any more. But getting back to you, Jane Browne. You seemed capable of arousing all my emotions, from tenderness to anger, and I wasn't sure that I liked it. You turned down my offer of a riding school, disobeyed all my instructions. Not even so very willing to accept a gift. Then, when I saw you that day on the moors, up on Hammond, I could cheerfully have murdered you! '

' Instead,' Jane's lips curved in a reflective smile, ' you kissed me. Did you ever suspect that I was holding

188

something back?'

'You didn't on that occasion,' he teased cruelly, watching with flickering amusement the pink colour flare beneath her skin. 'I did suspect a few times, but when a man is falling in love he's inclined to turn a blind eye. But,' he went on emphatically, running his fingers through her long hair, taking a small handful of it, 'never try to deceive me again. When I'm your husband I don't mind telling you that I shall extract the most enjoyable forfeits.'

Completely acquiescent, yet still vulnerable to a small measure of feminine curiosity, Jane smiled but did not protest. Instead she asked tentatively, 'What did Daddy say when you told him we were to be married?'

Karl's eyes gleamed. 'He said, darling, that he was quite willing to give his blessing, and that I'd need it. But I assured him that I'd be more than able to cope. Once I get you back to High Linton you won't ever escape me again. And I refuse to wait long before doing just that.'

Jane sighed, unprotesting, in complete agreement as his lips descended. 'Darling Karl,' she whispered, minutes later, 'I only want you and High Linton. But most of all you, because I love you, always.'

The wind thrust hard against the window, flinging another shower of rain against the glass. Fast in Karl's arms, Jane didn't hear it as he caught her last words and echoed them urgently back against her lips.

Romances you have loved

Mills & Boon Best Seller Romances are the love stories that have proved particularly popular with our readers. They really are "back by popular demand." These are the other titles to look out for this month.

ERRANT BRIDE
by Elizabeth Ashton

Antoine de Mericourt was going to turn Sylvie into a great star of the ballet – which was why he had married her, just to ensure that no romantic distractions would interfere with her career. He had no intention of allowing the marriage to become a real one – but what about Sylvie's feelings?

A KISS FROM SATAN
by Anne Hampson

'Place your hand on a woman's heart and she's yours instantly,' said the arrogant Greek Julius Spiridon. Gale, embittered after being let down by the man she loved, had vowed never to let a man touch her heart again. So she was absolutely determined to fight the attraction she so unwillingly felt for Julius . . .

Mills & Boon

TOO YOUNG TO LOVE
by Roberta Leigh

Sara was only eighteen when she fell in love with Gavin Baxter – which was perhaps the reason why her stepmother had so easily made mischief and wrecked the affair. Now Sara was older and Gavin had come back into her life. Was she mature enough now to win his love a second time?

DARK VENETIAN
by Anne Mather

Emma ought to have known that her stepmother Celeste never did anything except for selfish reasons, and even a holiday in a Venetian *palazzo* could not compensate her for the heartache she was to suffer. Celese wanted to add a title to her wealth – but did it *have* to be Count Vidal Cesare, the man Emma herself loved?

THE SNOW ON THE HILLS
by Mary Wibberley

Vanessa was used to turning men's heads and contemplated no particular difficulties in dealing with the masterful Callum Grayne. But was she to find that, for once, she had bitten off more than she could chew? And why did it matter so much to her?

the rose of romance